"You planned this," she accused in a hushed tone, because her throat was working to swallow down her rising anger.

"I plan everything, Inez," he replied simply.

She looked into his face. The indomitable determination stamped on Theo's harsh features sent a wave of anxiety through her.

She started to speak, to say the words that seemed unreal to her, and her mouth trembled. His gaze dropped to the telling reaction, and she immediately clamped her lips together. Showing weakness would only get her eaten alive.

Not that she wouldn't be anyway. A bubble of hysteria threatened. She swallowed and held his gaze.

"You want me to be your *mistress*?"

His laugh was long and deep. "Is that what you would call yourself?"

She flushed. "How else would you describe what you've just demanded of me? This *keeping* me? What you're suggesting is archaic enough to be described as such. Or does *plaything* more suit your pseudomodernistic outlook?"

"No, Inez. I don't like the term *plaything* either. I have no intention of playing with you. No, what I foresee for us is much more grown-up than that." The sexual intent behind the statement was unmistakable.

Rather than being offended or shocked, Inez found herself growing breathless. Excited.

No!

"Yes," he murmured, as if he'd read her mind.

The Untamable Greeks

Rich, powerful and impossible to resist

Sakis, Arion and Theo Pantelides—three formidable brothers who have risen up from the darkness of their pasts to conquer the world. Powerful, gorgeous and fabulously wealthy, these deliciously arrogant Greeks can have any woman they want—but none will ever tame them.

Until now...?

WHAT THE GREEK'S MONEY CAN'T BUY
April 2014

Sakis is hungry to give in to the forbidden temptation of his buttoned-up PA—but will the cynical Greek pay the price for breaking his golden rule?

WHAT THE GREEK CAN'T RESIST
June 2014

Perla Lowell is the last woman Arion should want, and yet he can't deny himself one night with this irresistible temptress—but what will happen when this dark-hearted Greek discovers the consequences of succumbing to his desire?

WHAT THE GREEK WANTS MOST
December 2014

Business tycoon Theo Pantelides is in Brazil for one reason only—revenge. Bedding his enemy's beautiful socialite daughter, Inez da Costa, is an unexpected bonus—but will Theo's desire cost him more than he ever imagined?

Maya Blake

—

What The Greek Wants Most

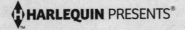

Recycling programs
for this product may
not exist in your area.

ISBN-13: 978-0-373-13300-0

What The Greek Wants Most

First North American Publication 2014

Copyright © 2014 by Maya Blake

This edition published by arrangement with Harlequin Books S.A.

For questions and comments about the quality of this book,
please contact us at CustomerService@Harlequin.com.

® and TM are trademarks of Harlequin Enterprises Limited or its
corporate affiliates. Trademarks indicated with ® are registered in the
United States Patent and Trademark Office, the Canadian Intellectual
Property Office and in other countries.

Printed in U.S.A.

All about the author...
Maya Blake

MAYA BLAKE fell in love with the world of the alpha male and the strong, aspirational heroine when she borrowed her sister's Harlequin® books at age thirteen. Shortly thereafter the dream to plot a happy ending for her own characters was born. Writing for Harlequin® is a dream come true. Maya lives in South East England with her husband and two kids. Reading is an absolute passion, but when she isn't lost in a book she likes to swim, cycle, travel and Tweet!

You can get in touch with her via email at mayablake@ymail.com, or on Twitter, @mayablake.

Other titles by Maya Blake available in ebook:

THE ULTIMATE PLAYBOY
  (The 21st Century Gentleman's Club)
WHAT THE GREEK CAN'T RESIST
  (The Untamable Greeks)
WHAT THE GREEK'S MONEY CAN'T BUY
  (The Untamable Greeks)
HIS ULTIMATE PRIZE

To my editor, Suzanne Clarke,
for your unfailingly brilliant insight and support!

CHAPTER ONE

THEO PANTELIDES ACCELERATED his black Aston Martin up the slight incline and screeched to a halt underneath the portico of the Grand Rio Hotel.

He was fifteen minutes late for the black tie fund-raiser, thanks to another probing phone call from his brother, Ari.

He stepped out into the sultry Rio de Janeiro evening and tossed the keys to an eager valet who jumped behind the wheel of the sports car with all the enthusiasm Theo had once felt for driving. For life.

The smile that had teased his lips was slowly extinguished as he entered the plush interior of the five-star hotel. Highly polished marble gleamed beneath his feet. Artistically positioned lighting illuminated the well-heeled and threw the award-winning hotel's design into stunning relief.

The hotel was by far the best of the best, and Theo knew the venue had been chosen simply because his hosts had wanted to show off, to project a false image to fool him. He'd decided to play along for now.

The right time to end this game would present itself. Soon.

A sleek designer-clad blonde dripping in diamonds clocked him and glided forward on sky-high stilettos, her strawberry-tinted mouth widening in a smile that spelled out a very feminine welcome. And more.

'Good evening, Mr Pantelides. We are so very honoured you could make it.'

The well-practised smile he'd learnt to flash on and off since he was eighteen slid into place. It had got him out of trouble more times than he could count and also helped him hide what he did not want the world to see.

'Of course. As the guest of honour, it would've been crass not to show up, no?'

She gave a little laugh. 'No, er, I mean yes. Most of the guests are already here and taking pre-dinner drinks in the ballroom. If there's anything you need, anything at all, my name is Carolina.' She sent him a look from beneath heavily mascaraed eyelashes that hinted that she would be willing to go above and beyond her hostess duties to accommodate him.

He flashed another smile. '*Obrigado*,' he replied in perfect Portuguese. He'd spent a lot of time studying the nuances of the language.

Just as he'd spent a lot of time setting up the events set to culminate in the very near future. For what he planned, there could be no room for misunderstanding. Or failure.

About to head towards the double doors that led to the ballroom, he paused. 'You said most of the guests are here. Benedicto da Costa and his family. Are they here?' he asked sharply.

The blonde's smile slipped a little. Theo didn't need to guess why. The da Costa family had a certain reputation. Benedicto especially had one that struck fear into the hearts of common men.

It was a good thing Theo wasn't a common man.

The blonde nodded. 'Yes, the whole family arrived half an hour ago.'

He smiled at her, effectively hiding the emotions bubbling beneath his skin. 'You've been very helpful.'

Her seductive smile slid back into place. Before she could grow bolder and attempt to ingratiate herself further, he turned and walked away.

Anticipation thrummed through his veins, as it had ever

since he'd received concrete evidence that Benedicto da Costa was the man he sought. The road to discovery had been long and hard, fraught with pitfalls and the danger of letting his emotions override his clear thinking.

But Theo was nothing if not meticulous in his planning. It was the reason he was chief troubleshooter and risk-assessor for his family's global conglomerate, Pantelides Inc.

He didn't believe in fate but even he couldn't dismiss the soul-deep certainty that his chosen profession had led him to Rio, and to the man who'd shattered what had remained of his tattered childhood twelve years ago.

Every instinct in his body yearned to take this to the ultimate level. To rip away the veneer of sophistication and urbanity he'd been forced to operate behind.

To claim his revenge. Here. Now.

Soon...

He grimaced as he thought of his phone call with his brother.

Ari was beginning to suspect Theo's motives for remaining in Rio.

But, despite the pressure from his family, neither Ari nor Sakis, his older brothers, would dare to stop him. He was very much his own man, in complete control of his destiny.

But that didn't mean Ari wouldn't try to dissuade him from his objective if he'd known what was going on. His oldest brother took his role as the family patriarch extremely seriously. After all, he'd had to step up after the secure family unit he'd known for his formative years had suddenly and viciously detonated from the inside out. After his father had betrayed them in the worst possible way.

Theo only thanked God that Ari's radar had been momentarily dulled by his newfound happiness with his fiancé, Perla, and the anticipated arrival of their first child.

No, he wouldn't be able to stop him. But Ari...was Ari.

Theo shrugged off thoughts of his family as he neared

the ballroom doors. He deliberately relaxed his tense shoulders and breathed out.

She was the first thing he saw when he walked in. His lips started to curl at his clichéd thought but then he realised she'd done it deliberately.

The dress code for this event had been strictly black and white.

She wore red. And not just any red. Her gown was blood-red, provocatively cut, and it lovingly melded to her figure in a way that made red-blooded males stop and stare.

Inez da Costa.

Youngest child of Benedicto. Twenty-four, socialite... seductress.

Against his will, Theo's breath caught as his gaze followed the supple curve of a breast, a trim waist and the flare of her hips.

He knew each and every last detail of the da Costas. For his plan to succeed, he'd had to do what he did best. Dig deep and extract every last ounce of information until he could recite every line in the six-inch dossier in his sleep.

Inez da Costa was no better than her father and brother. But where they used brute force, blackmail and thuggery, she used her body.

He wasn't surprised lesser men fell for her Marilyn Monroe figure. A true hourglass shape was rare to find these days. But Inez da Costa owned her voluptuousness and confidently wielded it to her advantage. Theo's gaze lingered on her hips until she moved again, dropping into conversation with the consummate ease of a practised socialite. She had guests eating out of her hands, leaning in close to catch her words, following her avidly when she moved away.

As he advanced further into the room, she turned to speak to another male guest. The curve of her bottom swung into Theo's eye line, and he cursed under his breath as heat raced up through his groin.

Hell, no.

His fists curled, willing his body's unwanted reaction away. It had been a while since he'd indulged in a mindless, no-holds-barred liaison. But this was most definitely not the time for a physical reminder, and the instigator of that reminder was most definitely not the woman he would choose to end his short dry spell with.

He exhaled in a slow, even stream, letting the roiling in his gut abate and his equilibrium return.

As he made his way down the stairs to join the guests, the deep-seated certainty that he was meant to be here—in the right place at the right time—flared high.

If Pietro da Costa's love of excess hadn't led him down the path of biting off more than he could chew, this time in the form of commissioning a top-of-the-line Pantelides super-yacht he could ill afford, Theo wouldn't have flown down to Rio to look into the da Costas' finances three years ago.

He wouldn't have become privy to the carefully hidden financial paper trail that had led right back to Athens and to his own father's shady dealings almost a decade and a half ago.

He wouldn't have dug deeper and discovered the consequences of those dealings for his family. And for him personally.

Memory stirred the unwanted threads of anxiety until it threatened to push its way under his control like Japanese knotweed. Gritting his jaw, he smashed down on the poisonous emotion that had taken too much from him already. He was no longer that frightened boy unable to stem his fears or chase away the screaming nightmares that plagued him.

He'd learned to accept them as part of his life, had woven them into the fabric of his existence and in doing so had triumphed over them. Which wasn't to say he wasn't determined to make those who'd temporarily taken power from him pay dearly for that error. No, that mission he was very much looking forward to.

Focusing his gaze across the room to where Benedicto and his son held court among Rio's movers and shakers, he strategised how best to approach his quarry.

Despite the suave exterior he tried to portray with his tailor-made suit and carefully cropped hair, Benedicto could never mask his lizard-like character for very long. His sharp, angular face and reptilian eyes held a cruelty that was instinctively felt by those around him. And Theo knew that he honed that characteristic to superb effect when needed. He bullied when charm failed, resulting in the fact that half of the people in this room had attended the fund-raiser tonight just to stay on Benedicto's good side.

Five years ago, Benedicto had made his political aspirations very clear, and since then he'd been paving the way for his rise to power through mostly unsavoury means.

The same unsavoury means Theo's own father had used to bring shame and devastation to his family.

Grabbing a glass of champagne, Theo sipped it as he slowly worked his way deeper into the room, exchanging pleasantries with ministers and dignitaries who were eager to find favour with the Pantelides name.

He noticed the moment Benedicto and Pietro zeroed in on his presence. Bow ties were surreptitiously straightened. Smiles grew wider and spines straighter.

He suppressed a smile, deliberately turned his back on the father and son and made a beeline for where the daughter was smiling up at Alfonso Delgado, the Brazilian millionaire philanthropist, who was her latest prey.

'If you want me to host a gala for you, Alfonso, all you have to do is say the word. My mother used to be able to throw events like these together in her sleep and I've been told that I've inherited her talent. Or do you doubt my talents?' Her head tilted in a coquettish move that most definitely would've made Theo snort, had his eyes not been drawn to the sleek line of her smooth neck.

Alfonso smiled, his expression beginning to closely resemble adoration.

Forcing himself not to openly grimace, Theo took another sip of champagne and brushed off an acquaintance who tried to catch his eye.

'No one in their right mind would doubt your talent. Perhaps we can discuss it over dinner one night this week?'

The smile that started to curve her full, glossy lips forced another punch of heat through him. 'Of course, I would love to. We can also discuss that pledge you made to support my father's campaign...?'

Theo moved closer, deliberately encroaching on the space between the two people in the centre of the room.

Alfonso's attention jerked towards him and his smile changed from playboy-charming to friendly welcome.

'*Amigo*, I wasn't aware that you had returned to my beloved country. It seems we cannot keep you away.'

'For what I need to achieve in Rio, wild horses couldn't keep me away,' he replied, deliberately keeping himself from glancing at the woman who stood next to Alfonso. He breathed in and caught her scent—expensive but subtle, a seductive whisper of flowers and warm sunshine.

His friend's eyes gleamed. 'Speaking of horses—'

Theo shook his head. 'No, Alfonso, your racehorses don't interest me. Speedboat racing, on the other hand... Just say the word and I'll kick your ass from one end of the Copacabana to the other.'

Alfonso laughed. 'No can do, my friend. Everyone knows underneath that tuxedo you're part shark. I prefer to take my chances on land.'

A delicate clearing of a throat made Alfonso turn, a smile of apology appearing on his face as he slipped back into playboy mode. For the ten years that Theo had known him, Alfonso had had a weakness for curvy brunettes.

Inez da Costa had curves that required their own danger

signs. His friend risked being easy prey for whatever the da Costas had in mind for him.

'Apologies, *querida*. Please allow me to introduce you to—'

Theo stopped him with a firm hand on his shoulder. 'I'm perfectly capable of making my own introductions. Right now, I think you're needed elsewhere.'

Alfonso's eyes widened in confusion. 'Elsewhere?'

Theo leaned and whispered in his friend's ear. Shock and anger registered on Alfonso's face before his jaw clenched and he reined his emotions back in. His gaze slid to the woman next to him and returned to Theo's.

Taking in a deep breath, he held out his hand. 'I guess I owe you one, my friend.'

Theo took the proffered hand. 'You owe me several, but who's counting?'

'And I shall repay you. *Até a próxima*.'

'Until next time,' Theo repeated. He heard the disbelieving gasp from Inez da Costa as Alfonso walked away without another glance in her direction.

A thread of satisfaction oozed through him as he tracked his friend to the ballroom doors. Scanning the room, he saw Pietro da Costa's thunderous look in his sister's direction.

Theo lifted his glass to his lips and took a lazy sip then turned his attention to Inez da Costa.

Her large brown eyes were filled with anger as she glared at him.

'Who the devil are you and what did you say to Alfonso?'

CHAPTER TWO

THEO DIDN'T LIKE the idea that he'd been less than one hundred per cent thorough in covering every angle in his investigations.

His surveillance of Inez da Costa had been from afar simply because until recently he'd deemed her involvement in his investigation peripheral at best.

The extent of her role in her father's organisation had only come to light a few days ago. But even then he should've recognised her power.

Now, at the first proper sight of what was turning out to be the jewel in Benedicto da Costa's crown, the essential cog in the sinister wheel that his enemy was intent on using to his full advantage, he experienced a pulse of heat so strong, so powerful, he sucked in a quick breath.

Up close, Inez da Costa's heart-shaped face was flawless…breathtaking, her skin a silky, vibrant complexion even the best cosmetics couldn't hope to produce.

Not that she hadn't attempted to enhance her beauty even further. Her make-up was impeccable, her lids smoky in a way that drew attention to her wide, doe-like stare.

Long-lashed eyes that bored into him with unwavering demand and a healthy dose of suspicion. Her nose flared with pure Latin ire and her full lips parted as she released another agitated breath.

The pictures in his dossier did her no justice at all. Flesh and blood wrapped in red silk from cleavage to toe, she made his senses ignite in a way he hadn't felt in a long time. The earlier pull deep in his groin returned. Harder.

'I asked you a question.' Her voice held a hint of dark sultriness that reminded him of a warm Santorini evening spent drinking ouzo on a deserted beach. And the mouth that framed her words, painted a deep matt red, reminded him of what happened on the beach after the ouzo had been consumed and inhibitions were at their loosest.

She glanced over his shoulder and Theo's jaw clenched at the thought that she was more concerned with the departing Alfonso than she was with him.

'Why is one of my guests walking out the door right this moment?'

'I told him that if he didn't want a noose slipped around his neck before he was ready to be hog-tied, he needed to stay away from you.'

Her parted mouth gaped wider, showing a row of perfect white teeth. *'Excuse me—?'*

'You're excused.'

Eyes the colour of dark caramel flashed. 'How dare you refer to me as such—?'

'Careful, *anjo*, you're causing a scene. *Pai* would not be happy to see his event ruined by a tantrum now, would he?'

Her eyes didn't stray from his, her stare direct and cutting in a way that made it difficult for him to look away. Or maybe it was because, despite the boldly challenging stare, he spied a quickly hidden vulnerability that tweaked his radar?

'I don't know who you think you are but perhaps you need to be educated in the etiquette of social gatherings. You don't deliberately set out to insult your host or—'

'My intention was quite simple. I wanted to get rid of the competition.'

'The *competition?*'

The doors to the larger ballroom where the dinner fund-raiser was to be held were thrown open. Theo turned to her. 'Yes. And now Alfonso's gone, I have you all to myself. And, as to who I am, I'm Theo Pantelides, your VIP guest of honour. Maybe you should add another bullet point to your rules of etiquette. That the hostess should know who her most important guests are?'

Her mouth started to drop open but she caught her reaction and pursed her lips.

'You're Theo Pantelides?' she muttered.

'Yes, so I suggest you make nice with me to stop me from leaving. One high net worth guest departing before dinner may be excusable. Barely. Two will certainly not go down well with your crowd. Now, smile and take my arm.'

Inez reeled under the steely punch packed behind the suave, sophisticated exterior and charming smile.

Theo Pantelides.

This was the man her father and Pietro had talked about. The one who would be taking over majority shares in Da Costa Holdings until after the elections. The one her brother Pietro had referred to as an arrogant bastard.

Well, he certainly was arrogant all right. The swiftness with which he'd dispatched Alfonso and assumed he could control her confirmed that assertion. As to whether he was a true bastard...well, that was something to be determined. But so far all signs pointed in that direction.

What she hadn't been aware of was that the man spoken of with such scorn would be so...visually breathtaking.

'I thought you would be older.' The words tripped from her tongue before she could stop herself.

'As opposed to young, virile and unbelievably handsome?' he drawled.

Shock jolted though her at his unapologetic, irritatingly justified confidence. Because he undeniably was. A full head of vibrant jet-black hair was common enough among her countrymen. Even his hazel eyes, sculpted cheekbones and square jaw were conventional in the polo-loving jet set crowd her father and brother encouraged her to associate with.

On this man, though, the whole combination had been elevated several hundred notches to an entirely different level of magnetism that demanded attention and got it. There was a quality about the way he carried himself, his broad shoulders unyielding, that spelled a tough inner core anyone would be foolish to mess with.

And yet that danger Inez could feel rising off him was... compelling. Alluring.

She found her gaze drifting over his face, past the tiny dimple in his chin to the dark bronze throat as he lazily swallowed a mouthful of champagne.

She inhaled a sharp dart of air as she watched his Adam's apple move. Then jerked back when her fingers flexed suddenly with the urge to touch him there.

Santa Maria!

She fought to remember her anger at this stranger. As much as she detested her role in tonight's events—the blatant begging for campaign funds disguised as a charity event—she couldn't let opportunities slip through her fingers.

It was the deal she'd made with her father.

An education in return for serving her time. In six short weeks she would be free to pursue her dreams. Free of her father's influence, of the sleazy, horrifying rumours that had been part of her childhood and what had driven her mother to quiet despair when she thought she wasn't being observed.

She needed to focus, not moon over how coarse this arrogant stranger's faintly stubbled jaw would feel against her skin.

'*Make nice?* After you rudely interrupted my conversation and sent my guest for the evening running without so much as a goodbye?'

'Think about that for a minute. Do you really want a man who would abandon you so easily on the strength of a few whispered words?'

Genuine anger replaced the momentary sensory aberration. 'That you needed to whisper those words instead of state them in my hearing makes me wonder just how confident you are of your manhood.'

Inez was used to being the butt of male jokes. Pietro and her father had mocked and dismissed her career ambitions until the day she'd picked up her suitcase and threatened to leave home for good.

But she was still shocked when the man in front of her threw back his head and laughed. Even more so when the sight of his strong white teeth and the genuine twinkling merriment in his eyes sent her pulse racing. An alien tingling started in her belly and spread outward like fractured lightning.

'Did I say something funny?'

Light hazel eyes speared hers. 'I've been challenged on a lot of things, *querida*, but never over my manhood.'

The political career her father so desperately craved produced men who could fake confidence with the best of them. She'd seen political candidates on a clear losing streak fake bravado until they were on the verge of looking totally ridiculous.

This man oozed confidence and power so very effortlessly it was like a second skin. Couple those two elements with the dangerous magnetism she could feel and Theo Pantelides was positively lethal.

Over her thundering heartbeat, she heard the master of ceremonies announce that the fund-raiser she'd so carefully orchestrated—the platform that would see her achieve her freedom—was about to begin.

Beyond one broad shoulder of the man who seemed to have sucked the air from the large ballroom, she saw her father and Pietro heading towards her.

Her father would want to know what had happened to Alfonso. The Brazilian businessman had promised to host a polo match on his large ranch where he bred the finest thoroughbreds. Securing a time and a date and a campaign donation had been her job tonight.

A much needed win this man had cost her.

Frustrated anger flared anew.

'This can be resolved very easily, Inez,' Theo Pantelides murmured in her ear. His voice was deep. Alluring. To hear him use her given name, the version her half-American mother had so lovingly bestowed on her, made her momentarily lose her bearings. A state that worsened when his hot breath washed over her neck.

Barely managing to suppress a shiver, she snapped herself back into focus. 'Don't say my name. In fact, don't speak to me. Just...just go away!'

Inez knew she was on the verge of displaying childish behaviour but she needed to regroup quickly, find a solution to a situation that had been so cut and dried fifteen minutes ago.

She watched her father and brother approach and the dart of pain that resided beneath her breastbone twisted. For a long time she'd yearned for a connection with them, especially after *Mãe* had been so cruelly ripped from their lives following a fall from a racehorse a week before Inez's eighteenth birthday. But she'd soon realised that she was alone in the pain and loneliness brought on by the loss of the mother who'd been her everything. Pietro had been given no time to grieve before their father had stepped up his grooming campaign. As for Benedicto himself, he'd barely finished burying his wife before resuming his relentless pursuit of political power.

The only other male she'd foolishly thought was honourable had turned out to be just as ruthlessly power-hungry as the men in her family.

Constantine Blanco—one lesson well and truly learned.

'I see the rumours were false after all,' the man who loomed, large and imposing, in front of her drawled in that deep voice of his, capturing her attention so effortlessly.

She pushed down the bitterness that swirled through her at the thought of what she'd allowed to happen with Constantine. How low she'd sunk in her need for love and a desire for a connection.

'What rumours?' She infused a carelessness in her voice she was far from feeling.

'The ones that said you exhibit grace and charm with each bat of your eyelids. At the moment all I can see is a hellcat intent on scoring grooves into my skin.'

'Then I suggest you stay away from me. I wouldn't want to ruin your *unbelievably handsome* face now, would I?'

She hurried away from his magnetic presence towards where the tables had been set out with highly polished sterling silver cutlery and exquisitely cut crystal. At twenty thousand dollars a plate, the event was ostensibly to raise money for the children trapped within Rio's *favelas*, a cause dear to her heart.

Shame it had to be tainted with power-hungry sharks, mild threats to secure votes and…devastatingly handsome rogues with piercing hazel eyes who made her breath catch in a frighteningly exciting way…

The direction of her thoughts made her stumble lightly. Catching herself, she smiled at a guest who slid her a concerned glance.

Each table was set for eight. Her father had insisted their table was placed in the centre, where all eyes would be on them.

With Alfonso's unexpected departure, the empty seat would stick out like the proverbial sore thumb once the Secretary of State and his wife and the other power couple had taken their places.

She had no choice but to bump someone to the high table. All she needed to figure out was who—

'Staring at the empty seat will not make your departed guest suddenly reappear, *senhorita*,' the deep voice uttered from behind her.

That hot shiver swept up her spine again.

Before she could summon an appropriately scathing retort, her chair and the one bearing Alfonso's name were pulled back.

'What are you doing?' she demanded heatedly under her breath. She continued to stare down at the place setting, unwilling to look up into those hazel eyes. Something in their light depths made her hyperaware of her body, of her increased heartbeat. As if she was prey and he was the merciless predator.

It was preposterous. She didn't like it. But it was undeniable.

'Saving your skin. Now, smile and play along.'

'I'm not a puppet. I don't smile on command.'

'Try. Unless you want to spend the rest of the evening sitting next to the equivalent of an elephant in the ballroom?'

Something in his voice made her forget her vow not to look into his eyes. Something…peculiar. Her head snapped up before she could stop herself.

Their eyes clashed. And she found herself in that hyperaware state again. She forced herself to breathe through it. 'You created the very situation you now seem intent on fixing. Why don't you save us both time and state what your agenda is?'

A look passed over his face. Too quickly for her to decipher but whatever it was made her breath catch in a totally different way from before. Warning spiked the hairs on her nape.

'I merely want to redress the situation a little. And, as talented as you seem to think you are at hiding it, I can see my actions caused you distress. Let me help make it better.'

'So you cause me grief then swoop in to save me like a knight in shining armour?'

'I'm no one's knight, *senhorita*. And I prefer Armani to armour.'

He pointedly held out her seat.

Casting a swift glance around, Inez saw that they were attracting attention. Short of causing a scene, there was nothing she could do. Willing her facial muscles to relax into a cordial smile, she slowly sat down and watched as Theo Pantelides folded himself into the seat next to her.

He reached for his champagne at the same time as she reached for her water glass. The brush of his knuckle against her wrist made her jump.

'Relax, *anjo*. I've got this,' came the smooth, deep reassurance.

A hysterical laugh bubbled up her throat, curbed at the last minute by a cough. 'Pardon me if that assurance brings me very little comfort.'

He lifted the glass she'd abandoned and held it out to her. 'Tell me, what's the worst that could happen?'

She took the glass and stared into the sparkling water. The need to moisten her dry throat had receded. 'Believe me, the worst already has happened.'

For a long time she'd hidden from the truth—that her father had his heir, and she was a useless spare part.

Pain writhed through her and her breath grew shaky as her throat clogged with anger and bitterness.

'Get yourself together. Now isn't the time to fall apart. Trust me, Delgado may be a good friend but he has a wandering eye.' The hard bite to his tone cut a path through her emotions.

Setting the glass down, she faced him. 'I have been toyed with enough to last me a century, and I know your business here tonight has nothing to do with me, so do me a favour, *senhor*, and tell me straight—what do you want?' she whispered fiercely. She noted vaguely that her heartbeat was once again on rapid acceleration to sky-high. Her fingers shook and her belly churned with emotions she couldn't have named to save her life.

'First of all, cut out the *senhor* bit. If you want to address me in any way, call me Theo.'

'I will address you how I see fit, Mr Pantelides. And I see that once again you have failed to give me a straight answer.'

'No, I've failed to jump when you say. You need to be taught a little patience, *anjo*.'

She lifted a deliberately mocking brow. 'And you propose to be the one to teach me?'

That wide, breathtaking smile appeared again. Just like that, her pulse leapt then galloped with a speed even the finest racehorse would've strained to match.

What was going on here?

'Only if you ask nicely.'

She was searching for an appropriately cutting response when her father reached the table with the rest of the guests.

He cast her a narrow-eyed glance before his gaze slid to Theo Pantelides.

'Mr Pantelides, I had hoped for a few minutes of your time before the evening started properly,' her father said as he took his seat across the table.

Inez wasn't sure whether she imagined the slight stiffening in the posture of the man beside her. Her senses were too highly strung for her to trust their accuracy. Searching his profile as he stared at her father, nothing in his face gave any indication as to his true feelings.

'I'm all for mixing business with pleasure. However, I draw the line at mixing business with the plight of the poor. Let the *favela* kids have their cause heard. *Then* we will attend to business.'

The firm put-down sent an arctic chill around the table. The Secretary's wife gave a visible gasp and her skin blanched beneath her overdone make-up. Pietro, who'd just approached the table as Theo replied, gripped the back of his chair, anger embedded in his face.

Silence reigned for several fraught seconds. Her father flicked a glance at Pietro, who yanked back his seat and sat down. The hands her brother placed on the table were curled into fists and for a moment Inez wondered if his famous temper was about to be let loose on their guests.

Benedicto smiled at Theo. 'Of course. This cause is extremely dear to my heart. My own mother was brought up in the *favelas*.'

'As indeed you were, no?' Theo queried silkily.

Again, the Secretary's wife gasped. She reached for her wine glass and took a quick gulp. When she went to take another, her husband surreptitiously stayed her hand and sent her a stern disapproving look.

Her father nodded to the waiter, who stood poised with a bottle of the finest red wine. He took his time to savour his first sip before he answered.

'You are quite mistaken, Mr Pantelides. My mother managed to escape the fate most of her lot failed to and bettered her life long before she bore me. But I inherited her fighting spirit and her determination to do what I can for the bleak place she once called home.'

Theo's eyebrow quirked. 'Right. I may have been misinformed, then,' he said, although his dry tone suggested otherwise.

'I assure you misinformation is rife when it comes to the ploys of political opponents. And I have been told more than once that only a foolish man believes everything he reads in the papers.'

Theo slashed a smile that had a definite edge to it across the table. 'Trust me, I know a thing or two about what lengths newspapers will go to achieve a headline.'

'We seem to have lost Alfonso. Would you care to explain his absence, Inez?' Pietro's voice slid through the conversation.

Anger still rippled off him and Inez was acutely aware that he hadn't directly addressed Theo Pantelides.

Before she could speak, the man in question turned to her brother. 'He was called away suddenly. Emergency business elsewhere. Couldn't be helped. Since I was there when he took his leave, your sister offered me his seat and I graciously accepted, didn't you, *anjo*?'

She saw Pietro's eyes visibly widen at the blatant endearment. Just as swiftly, they narrowed and she could almost see the wheels spinning in a different direction as his gaze swung between her and Theo Pantelides.

No! Never! Her fingers curled into fists and she glared at him until he looked away.

'Well, perhaps Delgado's loss is our gain, *sim*?' her father prompted.

Again Theo smiled. Again her heart thudded hard at the sheer magnetism of his smile, even though it sorely lacked any humour.

The man was an enigma. He'd inveigled his way onto the top table, then proceeded to insult his host, just as he'd insulted her.

Inez had little doubt her father would unleash his anger at the slight later.

But right now she was more puzzled by the man next to her. What was his game plan? If he was in a position to acquire a controlling share of their company then clearly he was a man of considerable means. But he wasn't Brazilian. That much she knew. So why was he interested in her father's political ambitions?

She realised she was staring when that proud head turned and gold-flecked hazel eyes captured hers, one eyebrow quirked in amusement.

Hastily averting her gaze, she picked up her glass and took another sip.

Thankfully, the master of ceremonies chose that moment to climb onto the podium to announce the first course and the first speaker.

Inez barely tasted the salmon mousse and the wine that

accompanied it. Nor did she absorb the speech given by the
health minister about what was being done to help the poor.

Her hyperawareness of the man beside her interfered
with her ability to think straight. The last time she'd felt anything remotely like this, she'd wandered down a path she'd
hated herself for ever since. She'd almost given herself to
a man who had no use for her besides using her as a pawn.

Never again!

Six more weeks. She needed to focus on that. Once her
father was on his campaign trail, she could start her new life.

She'd heard the rumours about her father's ruthless be-
ginnings when she was growing up; a couple of her school
friends had whispered about unsavoury dealings her father
had been involved in. Inez had never found concrete proof.
The one time she'd asked her mother, she'd been quickly
admonished not to believe lies about her family.

At the time, she'd assured herself that they weren't true.
But the passage of time had whittled away that assurance.
Now, with each day that passed, she suspected differently.

'You look as if the world is coming to an end, *anjo*,'
the man she was desperately trying to ignore murmured.
Again the endearment rolled off his tongue in a deep, seductive murmur that sent shivery awareness cascading over
her skin.

'I hope you're not going to ask me to smile again, because—' She gasped as he took her hand and lifted it to
his mouth.

Firm, warm lips brushed her skin and Inez's stomach
dipped in sensual free fall that took her breath away. Desperately, she tried to snatch her hand back.

'What the hell do you think you're doing?' she snapped.

'Helping you. Relax. If you continue to look at me like
you want to claw my eyes out, this won't work.'

'What exactly *is* this? And why on earth should I play
along?'

'Your brother and father are still wondering why Delgado

left so abruptly. Do you want to suffer the third degree later or will you let me help you make it all go away?'

She eyed him suspiciously. The notion that there was something going on behind that smooth, charismatic façade didn't dissipate. In fact, it escalated as he stared down at her, his features enigmatic save for that smile that lingered on his wide, sexy mouth.

'Why do you want to help me?' Again she tried to take back her hand but he held on, one thumb smoothing over her inner wrist. Blood surged through her veins at his touch, her pulse racing at the spot that he so expertly explored.

'Because I'm hoping it would persuade you to have lunch with me tomorrow,' he replied.

His gaze flicked across the table. Although his expression didn't change, she again sensed the tension that hovered on the edge of his civility. This man didn't like her family. Which begged the question: what was he doing here investing in their company?

He swung that intense stare back to her and she lost her train of thought. Grabbing it back, she shook her head.

'I'll have to refuse the lunch offer, I'm afraid. I have other plans.'

'Dinner, then?'

'I have plans then, too. Besides, don't you have business with my father tomorrow?'

'Our business won't take longer than me signing on a dotted line.'

'A dotted line that gives you a permanent controlling share in my family's company?'

His eyes gleamed. 'Not permanent. Only until I have what I want.'

CHAPTER THREE

'AND WHAT IS it you want?'

'For now? Lunch. Tomorrow. With you.' Another pass of his thumb over her pulse.

Another roll of sensation deep in her belly. The temptation to say yes suddenly overcame her, despite the warning bells shrieking at the back of her mind.

She forced herself to heed those warning bells. Her painfully short foray into a relationship had taught her that good looks and charm often hid an agenda that would most likely not benefit her or her heart. And Theo Pantelides had metaphorical skull and crossbones stamped all over him.

'The answer is still no,' she replied, a lot sharper than she'd intended.

His lips compressed but he shrugged. As if her answer hadn't fazed him.

And it probably hadn't. He was one of those men who drew women like bees to pollen. He could probably secure a lunch date with half of the women in this room and tempt the other married half into sin should he choose to.

With his dark, exquisite looks and deep sexy voice, he could have any woman he chose to display even the mildest interest in.

The thought that he would do just such a thing punched so fierce a reaction in her belly that she suppressed a shocked gasp.

What on earth is wrong with me? She needed to get herself back under control before she did something foolish—like discard her plans for tomorrow in favour of spending more time with this infuriatingly self-assured, visually stunning man.

Giving herself a fierce pep talk, she pulled her hand from his grasp.

She folded her hand in her lap and wrapped her other hand over her wrist. But suddenly her own touch felt…inadequate.

She was saved from exploring the peculiar feeling when the lights dimmed and the projector started reeling pictures of miles and miles of rusted shingle roofs that formed the world famous Rio *favelas*.

Her father climbed onto the podium to begin his speech.

The tale of despair-driven prostitution, violence, gang warfare and kidnapping of innocents, and the need to do whatever was needed to help was one she'd heard at many fund-raisers and charity dinners.

She clenched her fist. Knowing that half the people in here, dripping in diamonds and tuxedos worth several thousand dollars, would've forgotten the plight of the *favela* residents by the time dessert was served made her silently scream in frustration.

The need to get up, to walk out almost overwhelmed her but she stayed put.

There would be no running. No walking away from the work she'd committed herself to, nor walking away from the formative minds that were depending on her.

Fierce pride tightened her chest at the part she was playing in the young lives under her charge. And the fact that she'd managed to change that part of her own life without her father or brother's interference.

She refocused as her father finished his speech to rousing applause. The projector was shut off and the lights grew brighter.

She reached forward for her glass of wine and noticed that she was once again the focus of Theo's gaze.

'Should I be offended that I'm being so comprehensively ignored?' he asked.

'It's not a state you're used to, I expect?' With her surroundings once more in focus, she noticed the looks he was getting from women on other tables. She didn't delude herself that any of them were interested in his views on politics or world peace. No, each and every one of them would vie for much more personal, much more physical contact with the lean, broad-shouldered man next to her, whose hands casually caressed his wine glass stem in a way that made her think indecent thoughts.

She noticed the young famous actress on the next table where Theo should have been sitting gazing over at him, and again felt the sharp edge of an unknown emotion pierce her insides.

His smile grew hard. 'You'd be surprised.'

Curiosity brought her gaze back to his. 'Would I? How?'

'That question makes me think you've formed an opinion of me.'

'And that answer convinces me that you're very good at deflecting. You may fool others, but you do not fool me.'

He stared at her for a moment before one corner of his mouth lifted. Abruptly, he stood and held out his hand. 'Dance with me, *anjo*, and enlighten me further as to what you think you know about me.'

The demand was silky and yet implacable. In full view of the other guests, her refusal would be extremely discourteous.

Her heart hammered as she slowly slid her hand into his and let him draw her to her feet.

Emotions she was trying and failing to suppress flared up at the warmth and firmness of his grip. Fervently, she prayed for time to speed up, for the evening to end so she could be free of this man. Her reaction to him was puzzling in the extreme and the notion that she was being toyed with unsettled her more with each passing second.

As they skirted the table to head for the dance floor, her gaze met her father's. Expecting approval for accommodating the man whose business he was so obviously keen to garner, she was taken aback when she saw his icy disapproval.

Through the elite Rio grapevine she knew Alfonso Delgado's net worth and knew he couldn't afford to acquire a controlling share of Da Costa Holdings. So why did her father disapprove of a man who was clearly superior in monetary worth to Alfonso?

'You really have to do better with your social skills than this. Or I'll have to do something drastic to retain your attention.' The hard bite to Theo's voice slashed through her thoughts. 'Or were you really that into Delgado?'

'No, I wasn't.'

Her immediate denial seemed to pacify him. 'Then tell me what's on your mind.'

Inez found herself speaking before she could snap at him not to issue orders. 'Have you ever found yourself in a position where everything you do turns out wrong, no matter how hard you try?'

'There have been a few instances.' He pulled her close and slid an arm around her back. Heat transmitted to her skin via the soft material of her dress and flooded through her body. This close, his scent washed over her. Strong but not overpowering, masculine and heady in a way that made her want to draw even closer, touch her mouth to the bronze skin just above his collar.

Deus!

'You think this is one of those occasions for you?'

'I don't think; I know.'

'Why?'

Her laugh grated its way up her throat. 'Because I have a perfectly functioning brain.'

'You're worried because your father and brother are displeased with you?'

'Everything else this evening has gone according to plan except…'

'Delgado. You're worried that your father offered you up on a silver platter because he seems to think you're a prize worth winning and now he'll demand to know what you did wrong.'

Her eyes snapped to his, the insult surprisingly painful. 'What do you mean by *seems to think*? What do you know about my father? Or about me, for that matter?'

Theo forced himself not to tense at the question. Or let the fact that her body seemed to fit so perfectly in his arms impact on his thinking abilities. 'Enough.'

'Do you always go around making unfounded remarks about someone you've just met?'

He let a small smile play over his mouth. 'Enlighten me, then. Are you a prize worth winning?'

'There's no point enlightening you because it will serve no useful purpose. After tonight you and I will never meet again.'

She took a firm step back. Attempted to prise herself out of his arms. He held her easily, willing back the thrum of anger and bitterness that rose like bile in his throat.

'Never say never, *anjo*.'

Her fiery brown eyes glared at him. 'Don't.'

He feigned innocence. 'Don't what?'

'Don't keep calling me that.'

'You don't like it?'

'You have no right to slap a pet name on someone you just met.'

The hand holding hers tightened. 'Calm down—'

'No, I won't calm down. I'm not an angel. I'm certainly not *your* angel.'

'Inez.' A warning, subtle but effective.

Inez's pulse stalled, then thundered wildly through her veins.

'Don't,' she whispered again. Only this time she wasn't sure what she pleaded for.

He leaned closer until his mouth was an inch from her ear. When he breathed out, warmth teased her earlobe. 'Don't use your given name? It's either that or *anjo*. All the other words are only appropriate for the bedroom.'

Heat flamed through her belly as indecent thoughts of rumpled sheets, sweaty bodies and incandescent pleasure reeled through her mind.

She shook her head to dispel the images and heard his low laugh.

When she stared up at him, his eyes blazed down at her with a hunger that smashed through her body. Her nipples slowly hardened and the fire raged higher as his lips parted on another heart-stopping smile. Unable to help herself, her eyes dropped to the sensual curve of his mouth.

'I think it's my turn to say *don't*. Not if you don't want to be thrown over my shoulder and raced to the nearest cave.'

She forced a laugh despite the sensations rushing through her. 'This is the twenty-first century, *senhor*.'

'But what I'm feeling right now isn't. It's very basic. Primeval, in fact.'

He swerved her out of the path of another couple and used the move to draw her even closer. At the fierce evidence of his arousal against her stomach, Inez swallowed hard.

Her confusion escalated.

Constantine had been charismatic and breathtaking in his own right. But he'd never made her feel like *this*, not even in the beginning…before everything had gone disastrously wrong.

Thinking of the man who'd broken her heart and betrayed her so cruelly threw much needed ice over her heated senses. She'd made a fool of herself over one man. Foolishly believed he was the answer to her prayers. She was wise enough now to know Theo Pantelides wasn't the answer to any prayer, unless it was the crash and burn type.

'I believe I've fulfilled my obligatory dance duty to you. Perhaps you'd like to find a more unwitting female to club over the head and drag to your cave?' She injected as much indifference into her voice as possible.

'That won't be necessary. I've already found what I'm looking for.'

Theo watched several emotions chase over her features before Inez da Costa regained her impeccable hostess persona.

Although he silently cursed himself for his physical reaction, he was thankful she realised her effect on him.

Let her think she held the power. Allow her to believe that he could be manipulated to her advantage. Or, rather, her father's advantage.

Her reaction to Delgado's departure had shown him that fulfilling her role as her father's Venus flytrap was most important to Inez da Costa. Or was it something else? Did she hope to bag *herself* a millionaire while serving her father's purpose? She came from a family ruthless in its pursuit of wealth and power. Was that her underlying agenda?

That knowledge demanded that he rethink his strategy. The conclusion he'd arrived at was surprising but easily adaptable.

He had an opportunity to kill a few more birds with one stone. With any luck, he would conclude his business in Rio in a far shorter time than he'd already anticipated if he played his cards right.

Inez tried to wrench herself from his grasp once more. The primitive feelings he'd mentioned so casually a moment ago resurfaced. When she tugged harder, he forced himself to release her. Her soft hand slid from his, leaving a trail of sensation that made his groin pound and his blood heat.

The plan he'd hatched solidified as he gazed down into

her heart-shaped face, saw her fighting to stop her clear agitation from messing with her breathing.

Theo hid a smile.

Either she was offended at his primitive declaration or she was turned on by it. Since she wasn't slapping his face, he concluded that it was the latter.

His gaze dropped lower, and the sight of her tightly beaded nipples against her gown made his own breathing stall in his chest. Lower still, her tiny waist gave way to those tempting hips that his palms ached to explore.

Even as he talked himself into believing his reaction would ultimately serve his purpose, a part of Theo was forced to acknowledge that he hadn't reacted this strongly to a woman in a very long time. Everything about her brought his senses to roaring life in a way only the thought of re-venge had for the past decade.

Revenge...retribution over the person who had created such chaos in his life.

He gritted his teeth as the sound of tinkling laughter and animated conversation refocused his mind to his task and purpose.

'Good evening, Mr Pantelides. I hope you enjoy the rest of your evening,' Inez said stiltedly.

She turned and walked off the dance floor before he could reply. Not that he felt like replying. Although he'd mostly kept on track throughout the evening, a large part of him had become far too consumed by her seductive pres-ence.

Inez da Costa was only one part of the game. To keep on track he needed to keep his head in the *whole* game.

He headed for the bar and sensed the moment Benedicto and his son halted their conversation and moved pincer-like towards him.

Dreaded anxiety washed over his senses but he forced himself to breathe through it.

I am no longer in that dark, cold place. I am in light. I am free...

He tersely repeated the short statement under his breath as he tossed back the shot of vodka and set it down with cold, precise care.

He was no longer weak. No longer helpless.

And he most certainly would never be put in a position to beg for his life. Ever again.

By the time they reached him, he'd regained control of his body.

'Senhor Pantelides—'

'We're about to become business partners—' his gaze slid over Pietro's head to where Inez was holding court in a group of guests; the sleek line of her neck and the curve of her body sent another punch of heat straight to his groin '—and hopefully a little bit more than that. Call me Theo.'

The younger man looked a little taken aback, but he rallied quickly, nodded and held out his hand. 'Theo...we wanted to hammer down a time to discuss finalising our agreement.'

He took Pietro's hand in a firm grip. Benedicto started to offer his hand. Theo deliberately turned away. Catching the bartender's eye, he held up his fingers for three more drinks. By the time he faced them again, Benedicto had lowered his hand.

Theo breathed through the deep anger that churned through his belly and smiled.

'Tomorrow. Ten o'clock. My office. I'll have the documents ready for us to sign.'

This time it was Benedicto who looked taken aback. 'I was under the impression that you wanted to iron out a few more details.'

Theo's gaze flicked back to Inez. 'I had a few concerns but they no longer matter. Your campaign funds will be ready in the next twenty-four hours.'

Father and son exchanged triumphant looks. 'We are pleased to hear it,' Benedicto said.

'Good, then I hope the three of you will join me for dinner tomorrow evening to celebrate our new deal.'

Benedicto frowned. 'The three of us?'

'Of course. I expect that, since this is a family company, your daughter would wish to be included in the celebrations? After all, the company was her mother's family's business before it became yours, Senhor da Costa, was it not?' he queried silkily.

The older man's eyes narrowed and something unpleasant slid across his face. 'I bought my father-in-law out over a decade ago but yes, it's a family business.'

Bought out using money he'd obtained by inflicting pain and merciless torment.

The bartender slid their shots across the polished counter.

Theo picked up the nearest shot glass and raised it. 'In that case, I look forward to welcoming you all as my guests tomorrow evening. *Saúde.*'

'*Saúde,*' Benedicto and his son responded.

Theo threw back the drink and this time didn't hold back from slamming it down.

Again he saw father and son exchange looks. He didn't care.

All he cared about was making it out of the ballroom in one piece before he buried his fist in Benedicto da Costa's bony face. The urge to tear apart the man who'd caused his family, caused *him*, so much anguish reared through him.

The sound of his phone vibrating in his jacket pocket brought a welcome distraction from his murderous thoughts.

'Excuse me, gentlemen.' He walked away without a backward glance, gaining the double doors leading out to the wide terrace before activating his phone.

'Heads up, you're about to get into serious trouble with Ari if you don't fess up as to why you're really in Rio,' Sakis, his brother, said in greeting.

'Too late. I've already had the hairdryer treatment earlier this evening.'

'Yeah, but do you know he's thinking of flying down there for a face-to-face?'

Theo cursed. 'Doesn't he have enough on his hands being all loved up and taking care of his pregnant fiancé?' He wasn't concerned about a confrontation with Ari. But he was concerned that Ari's presence might alert Benedicto to Theo's true intentions.

So far, Benedicto da Costa was oblivious as to the connections Theo had made to what had happened twelve years ago. The older man had been very careful to erase every connection with the incident and sever ties with anyone who could bear witness to the crime he'd committed. He hadn't been careful enough. But he didn't know that.

Having another Pantelides in Rio could set off alarm bells.

'You need to stall him.'

'He's concerned,' Sakis murmured. Theo heard the same concern reflected in his brother's voice. 'So am I.'

'It needs to be done,' he replied simply.

'I get that. But you don't need to do it alone. He's dangerous. The moment he guesses what your true intentions are—'

'He won't; I've made sure of it.'

'How can you be absolutely certain? Theo, don't be stubborn. I can help—'

'No. I need to see this through myself.'

Sakis sighed. 'Are you sure?'

Theo turned slowly and surveyed the ballroom. Rio's finest drank and laughed without a care in the world. In the centre of that crowd stood Benedicto da Costa, the reason why Theo couldn't sleep through a single night without waking to hellish nightmares; the reason anxiety hovered just underneath his skin, ready to infest his control should he loosen his grip for one careless second.

Inexorably, his eyes were drawn to the female member of the diabolical family. Inez was dancing with a man whose blatant interest and barely disguised lust made Theo's fist curl over the cold stone bannister.

His stomach churned and adrenaline poured through his system the same way a boxer experienced a heady rush in the seconds before a fight. This fight had been long coming. He would see it through. He had to. Otherwise he feared his demons would never be exorcised.

He'd lived with them for far too long, and they needed to be silenced. He needed to regain complete, unshakeable hold of his life once more.

His other hand tightened around his mobile phone, his heart thundering enough to drown out the music. He spoke succinctly so his brother would be in no doubt that he meant every word.

'Am I sure that I need to bring down the man who kidnapped and tortured me for over two weeks until Ari negotiated a two million ransom for my release? *Hell, yes*. I'm going to make him feel ten million times worse than what he did to me and to our family and I don't intend to rest until I bring all of them down.'

CHAPTER FOUR

'A DOUBLE-SHOT AMERICANO, *por favor.*' Inez smiled absently at the barista while she tried to juggle her sketchpad and fish out enough change from her purse to pay for the coffee.

It was barely nine o'clock and yet the heat was already oppressive, even more than usual for a Thursday morning in February. Normally, she would've opted for a cool caffeine drink but her energy levels needed an extra boost this morning.

She'd slept badly after the fund-raiser last night. And what little sleep she'd managed had been interspersed with images of a man she had no business thinking, never mind dreaming, about.

And yet Theo Pantelides's face had haunted her slumber...still haunted her, if truth be told.

The last time she'd seen him he'd been leaning against the terrace bannister outside the ballroom, his eyes fixed firmly on her. Inez wasn't sure why her attention had been drawn outside. All she knew was that something had compelled her to look that way as she danced with a guest.

Even from that distance the tension whipping through his frame had been unmistakable, as had the blatant dark promise in his eyes as his gaze raked her from head to toe.

More than anything she'd wished she could lip-read when she'd watched his lips move to answer whoever was at the other end of his phone conversation.

That last look plagued her. It'd held hunger, anger and another emotion that she couldn't quite decipher. Brushing it off, she smiled, accepted her coffee and headed outside. She was a little early for her class with the inner city kids but she hadn't wanted to spend another moment at the tension-fraught breakfast table with her father and brother this morning.

In contrast to Pietro's third degree as to what exactly had happened with Alfonso Delgado, her father had been cold and strangely preoccupied. The moment he'd stood abruptly and left the table, she'd made her excuses and walked away.

Even Pietro's reminder that they had a dinner engagement she couldn't recall making hadn't been worth stopping to query. All she'd wanted was to get out of the mansion that felt more and more as if it was closing in on her.

'*Bom dia, anjo.*' The deep murmured greeting brought her thoughts and footsteps to a crashing halt.

Theo leaned casually against a gleaming black sports car, a pair of dark sunglasses hiding his eyes from her. But her full body tingle announced that she was the full, unwavering focus of his gaze. Her breath stalled, her heart accelerating wildly as her pulse went into overdrive.

'What the hell are you doing here?' she blurted before she could stop her strong reaction.

Aside from the devastation his tall, lean suited frame caused to her insides, the thought that he could discover where she was headed or what she did with her Tuesday and Thursday mornings made her palms grow clammy. By lunchtime today, if Pietro were to be believed, Theo would be firmly entrenched as a business partner in her family's company. Which meant constant contact with her family. Which meant he could disclose parts of her life she wasn't yet ready to disclose to her family.

'Are you following me?' she accused hotly as she approached him, her senses jumping with the possibilities and consequences of her discovery.

'Not today. My trench coat and fedora are at the laundry.'

'Keep them there. In this heat, you'd boil to death.'

A smile broke across his face. 'Do I detect a little un-ladylike relish in your voice, *anjo*?'

'What you detect is high scepticism that you're here by accident and not following me,' she snapped.

'You give me too much credit, *agape mou*. I asked for the best coffee shop in the city and I was directed here. That you're here too merely confirms that assertion. Unless you go out of your way to sample bad coffee?'

Before she could respond, he straightened and reached for the hand wrapped around her coffee. Curling his hand over hers, he brought his lips to the small opening on her coffee lid and tilted the cup towards him.

He savoured the drink in his mouth for a few seconds before he swallowed.

Inez fought to breathe as she watched his strong throat move. The slow swirl of his tongue over his lower lip caused darts of sharp need to arrow straight between her legs.

'Delicious. And surprising. I would've pegged you for a latte girl.'

'Which goes to show you know next to nothing about me,' she retorted.

He slowly raised his sunglasses and speared her with his mesmerising eyes. Although a smile hovered over his sensual lips, some unnameable tension hovered in the air between them. A charged friction that warned her all was not as it seemed.

Hell, she knew that. Theo Pantelides spelled danger. Whether smiling or serious, dallying with him was akin to playing with electricity. Depending on his mood, you could either receive a mild static frizzle or a full-blown electro-cution. And she had no intention of testing him for either.

'*Sim*, I don't know enough about you. But I intend to remedy that situation in the near future.'

She shrugged. 'It is your time to waste.'

He merely smiled and turned towards his car.

'I thought you came to get coffee?' she probed, then bit her lip for prolonging a meeting she wanted over and done with. Last night she'd told herself to be thankful that she would never see this man again. And yet, here she was, feeling mildly bereft at the notion that he was leaving.

He paused and his gaze slid over her. Immediately, she became supremely conscious of the white shorts and blue tank top she'd hurriedly thrown on this morning. Her hair was caught up in a ponytail because it helped keep it out of the way during her class. Her face was devoid of make-up except for the light sunscreen and the gloss she'd passed over her lips. All in all, she projected a much different image this morning than the sophisticated hostess she'd been last night.

Catching herself wondering whether he found her wanting now, she mentally slammed the thought down. She didn't care what Theo thought of her.

'I have the kick I need to keep me going. See you tonight.'

'Tonight? Why would you be seeing me tonight?' she demanded.

His smile slowly disappeared as his gaze slid over her again. This time, his hot gaze held an element of possessiveness that made her fight to keep from fidgeting under his keen scrutiny.

Stepping back, he activated a button on his car key and the door slid smoothly upward. She watched, completely captivated, as he lowered his tall masculine frame inside the small space. A touch of a slim finger on a button and the engine roared to life.

'Because I want to see you. And I always get what I want, Inez,' he said cryptically, his tone suddenly hard and biting. 'Remember that.'

I always get what I want.

Another shiver of apprehension coursed down her spine. All through the two art and graphic design classes she taught from ten till midday, the infernal words throbbed through her head as if someone had set them on repeat.

She managed to keep her focus, barely, as she demonstrated the differences between charcoal and pencil strokes to a group of ten-year-olds. Once or twice she had to repeat herself because she lost her train of thought, much to the amusement of her pupils, but the satisfying feeling of imparting knowledge to children who would otherwise have been left wandering the streets momentarily swamped the roiling emotions that Theo had stirred with his unexpected appearance this morning.

The suspicion that he had been following her didn't go away all through her hurriedly taken lunch and the meeting she'd scheduled with the volunteer coordinator at the centre.

Her decision to forge her own path by seeking a permanent position at the centre had solidified as she'd tossed and turned through the night.

Seeking her independence meant finding a paying job. To do that she needed more experience, which she hoped her longer hours spent volunteering would give her.

Thanks to her father's interference, all she had was one semester at university. It wasn't great but, until such time as she could further her education, it was better than nothing. That plus her volunteering was a starting point.

A starting point that was greatly enhanced when the coordinator agreed to increase her hours to three full days.

She was smiling as she activated her phone on the way to her car after leaving the centre.

The first text was from Pietro, reminding her that they were dining out that evening. With Theo Pantelides.

The unladylike curse she uttered won her a severe look of disapproval from an elderly lady walking past. The urge to text back a refusal was immediate and visceral.

After last night and this morning, exposing herself to the raw emotions Theo provoked was the last thing she needed.

And even more than her suspicions this morning, she

had a feeling he'd engineered this dinner. Hell, he'd as much as taunted her with it with his last words to her this morning.

As much as she tried to think positive and hope that the dinner would be quick and painless, a premonition gripped her insides as she slid behind the wheel and headed home.

'Filho da puta.' Her brother's habitual crude cursing wasn't a surprise to her. That it had seemingly come out of nowhere was.

'What's wrong?' She eyed him as they stepped out of the car at the marina of the exclusive Rio Yacht Club just before seven p.m.

She pulled down her box-pleated hem and wished she'd worn something a little longer than the form-fitting mid-thigh-length royal-blue sleeveless dress. The traffic had been horrendous and she'd arrived home much later than planned. The dress had been the nearest thing to hand. Now she stared down at the four-inch black platform heels she'd teamed with it and grimaced at the amount of thigh and legs on show.

The light breeze lifted a few strands of her loose hair as she turned to her brother and saw him jerk his chin towards the largest yacht moored at the far end of the pier. 'Trust Pantelides to rub my nose in it,' he said acerbically.

She looked from the sleek black, gold-trimmed vessel back to her brother. 'Rub your nose…what are you talking about?'

With a sullen look, he strode off down the jetty. 'That's my boat.'

'*Yours*? When did you buy a boat?'

'I didn't. I couldn't. Not after the mess up with *Pai*'s last campaign. That boat was supposed to be mine!' Dark anger clouded his face.

Her heart jumped into her throat. 'Pietro, a boat like that costs millions of dollars. Besides that very unsubtle hint that

I in any way stood in the way of your acquiring it—which is preposterous, by the way—there's no way you could ever have afforded a boat like that, so—'

'Forget it. Let's go and get this over with. It's bad enough *Pai* pulled out of coming tonight. Now I have to schmooze for both of us. You have to play your part, too. It's clear Pantelides's got a thing for you.'

Disgust and anger rose in her and she snatched her hand away from Pietro when he tried to lead her down the gangplank.

'I won't participate in another of your soulless schemes. So you may as well forget it right now.'

'Inez—'

'No!' Feelings she'd bottled up for much longer than she cared to think about rose to the surface. 'You keep asking me to throw myself at prospective investors so you can fund *Pai*'s campaign. You're his campaign manager and yet you can't seem to function without my help. Why is that?'

Pietro's eyes darkened. 'Watch your mouth, sister.'

'Show me some respect and I'll consider it,' she challenged.

'What the hell has got into you?'

'Nothing that hasn't always been there, Pietro. But you need me to point it out to you so I will. I'm done. If you want me to accompany you as your *sister* to Theo Pantelides's dinner, then I will. If you have another scheme up your sleeve, then you might as well forget it because I am not interested.'

Her brother's lips pursed but she saw a hint of shame in his eyes before his gaze slid away. 'I don't have time to argue with you right now. All I ask, if it's not too much, of course, is that you help me secure this deal with Pantelides, because if we lose his backing then we might as well pack up and head back up to the ranch in the mountains.' He set off down the jetty.

She hurried to keep up, picking her way carefully over

wooden slats. 'But I thought everything was done and dusted this morning?' she asked when she caught up with him.

Anxiety slid over Pietro's face. 'Pantelides cancelled the meeting. Something came up, he said. Except I know it was a lie. I have it on good authority he was parked outside a coffee shop chatting up some girl when he was supposed to be meeting us to finalise the agreement.'

Inez stumbled, barely catching herself from toppling headlong into the water a few feet away.

'You're having him watched?' How she managed to keep her voice even, she didn't know.

Petulance joined anxiety. 'Of course I am. And I'd bet my Rolex that he's doing the same to us.'

The thought of being the subject of anyone's surveillance made her skin crawl, even though a part of her had reluctantly accepted the truth: that her father's business dealings weren't always legitimate. But hearing her brother admit it made her stomach turn.

And if that was the way Theo Pantelides conducted his business as well…

She pressed her lips together and looked up as Pietro strode past the potted palm lined entrance to the Yacht Club.

'Aren't we dining in there?'

He shook his head. 'No. We're dining on my…on *his* boat,' he tossed out bitterly.

Inez glanced at the yacht they were approaching.

This close, the vessel was even more magnificent. Its sleek lines and exquisite craftsmanship made her fingers itch for her sketching pad. She was so busy admiring the boat and yearning to capture its beauty on paper that she didn't see its owner until she was right in front of him.

Then everything else ceased to register.

He wore a black shirt with black trousers, his dark hair raked back from his face. Under the soft golden lights spilling from the second deck his sculpted cheekbones and strong jaw jutted out in heart-stopping relief.

At the back of her mind, Inez experienced a bout of irritation at the fact that he captured attention so exclusively. So effortlessly.

Even as he shook hands with Pietro and welcomed him on board the *Pantelides 9*, his eyes remained on her. And God help her, but she couldn't look away.

On unsteady feet, which she firmly blamed on the swaying vessel, she climbed the steps to where he waited. When his eyes released hers to travel over her body, she grappled with controlling her breath. She reached him and reluctantly held out her hand in greeting.

'Thank you for the dinner invitation, Mr Pantelides.'

With a mocking smile, he took her hand and used the grip to pull her close. Despite her heels, he was almost a foot taller than her, easily six foot four. Which meant he had to lean down quite a bit to whisper in her ear, 'So formal, *anjo*. I look forward to loosening your inhibitions enough to dissolve that starchy demeanour.'

Her pulse, which had begun racing when his palm slid against hers, thundered even harder at his words. 'I can see how not having a woman fall at your feet the moment you crook your finger can present a challenge, *senhor*. But you really should learn the difference between playing hard to get and being plainly uninterested.'

His eyebrow quirked. 'You fall into the latter category, of course?' he mocked.

'*Sim*, that is exactly so.'

He looked towards where Pietro had accepted a glass of champagne from a waiter and was admiring the luxuriously decorated deck, at the end of which a multi-coloured lit jet pool swirled and shimmered.

When his gaze re-fixed on hers, there was a steely determination in his eyes that sent a shiver down her spine. All the earlier alarm bells where Theo was concerned clanged loudly in her brain.

'Then I will have to get a little more inventive,' he murmured silkily before dropping her hand.

Inez clenched her fist and fought the urge to rub the tingling in her palm. She didn't want him getting inventive where she was concerned because she had a nasty feeling she wouldn't emerge unscathed from the encounter.

But she kept her mouth shut and followed him onto the deck. The cream and gold décor was the last word in luxury and opulence. Plump gold seats offered comfort and a superior view onto the well-lit marina and the open sea to their right. To their left, the lights of Rio gleamed, with the backdrop of the huge mountain, on top of which resided the world-famous Cristo Redentor.

A sultry breeze wafted through the deck as a waiter served more flutes of champagne. She took a glass as Pietro rejoined them. His glass was already half empty and she watched him take another greedy gulp before he pointed a finger at Theo.

'I wish you'd given me the chance to make you another offer for this boat before you pulled the plug on our sale agreement, Pantelides.'

Theo's jaw tightened before he answered. 'You had several opportunities to make good but you failed to close the deal. So I cut my losses.' He shrugged. 'Business is business.'

Pietro bristled. 'And cancelling our meeting today? Was that for business too, or pleasure?'

Theo's eyes caught and held hers. Inez held her breath, wondering if he was about to give her up. His eyes gleamed with a mixture of danger and amusement. Somehow he'd sensed that he held her in his power. And he relished that power. Her hand trembled slightly as she waited for the axe to fall.

'I'm not in the habit of discussing my other business interests, or my pleasurable ones, for that matter. But, suffice it to say, what kept me away from our meeting was very much worth my time.' His gaze swept down, lingering over her breasts and hips in a blatant appraisal that made her breathing grow shallow. When his eyes returned to hers, Inez was sure all the oxygen had been sucked out of the atmosphere.

'Our business together should be equally worth your time,' Pietro countered.

Theo finally set her free from his captivating gaze. Narrow-eyed, he glanced at Pietro.

'Which is why I rescheduled for this evening. Of course, your father chose not to grace us with his presence. So the song and dance continues, I guess.' The hard edge was definitely in his tone again, prompting those alarm bells to ring louder.

Pietro muttered something under his breath that she was sure wasn't complimentary. He snapped his fingers at the waiter and swapped his empty glass for a full one.

'Well, we'll be there at the appointed time tomorrow. We can only hope that you will not be delayed...elsewhere.'

The upward movement of Theo's mouth could in no way be termed a smile. His eyes flicked back to her. 'Don't worry, da Costa, I intend to hammer out the final points of our agreement tonight. When I turn up to sign tomorrow, it will be with the knowledge that all my stipulations have been satisfied.'

The firm belief that his statement was connected to her wouldn't dissipate all through dinner. As a host, Theo was effortlessly entertaining. He even managed to draw a chuckle from Pietro once or twice.

But Inez couldn't shake the feeling that they were being toyed with. And once or twice she caught the faintest hint of fury and repulsion on his face, especially when her father's name came up.

She shook herself out of her unsettling thoughts when the most mouth-watering dessert was set down before her.

Whatever Theo was up to, it was nothing to do with her. Her father had managed their family business with enough savvy not to be drawn into a scam.

With that comforting thought in mind, she picked up her spoon and scooped up a mouthful of chocolate truffle-topped cheesecake.

Her tiny groan of delight drew intense eyes back to hers. Suddenly, the thought of dishing out a little of the mockery he'd doled out to her tingled through her. Keeping her gaze on his, she slowly drew the spoon out from between her lips, then licked the remnants of chocolate with a slow flick of her tongue.

His nostrils flared immediately, hunger darkening his eyes to a leaf-green that was mesmerising to witness. With another swirl of her tongue, she lowered the spoon and scooped up another mouthful.

His large fist tightened around the after-dinner espresso he'd opted for and she momentarily expected the bone china to shatter beneath his grip. But slowly he released it and sat back in his chair, his eyes never leaving her face.

'Enjoying your dessert, *anjo*?' he asked in that low, rough tone of his.

She hated to admit that the endearment was beginning to have an effect on her. The way he mouthed it made heat bloom in her belly, made her aware of her every heartbeat... made her wonder how it would sound whispered to her at the height of passion. *No!*

'Yes. Very much.' She fake smiled to project an air of nonchalance.

He smiled at her mocking formality. 'Good. I'll make a note of it for the next time we dine together.'

Before she could tell him she intended to move heaven and earth to make sure there wouldn't be a next time, Pietro lurched to his feet. 'I never got the chance to inspect my…this boat before the opportunity to buy it was regrettably taken away. You won't mind if I take a look around, would you?' he slurred.

Theo motioned the hovering waiter over. He murmured to him and the waiter went to the deck bar and picked up a handset. 'Not at all. My skipper will give you the tour.'

A middle-aged man with greying hair climbed onto the deck a few minutes later and escorted a swaying Pietro towards the stairs.

Inez watched him go with a mixture of anxiety and sympathy.

'He's drunk.' Her appetite gone for good, she set her spoon down and pushed the plate away.

'You say that as if it's my fault,' he replied lazily.

'Did you really have to do that?' She glared at him.

He raised a brow. 'Do what, exactly?'

'This was supposed to be Pietro's boat.' No matter how unrealistic that notion had been, her brother didn't deserve to be humiliated like this.

'*Supposed* being the operative word. We had a *gentleman's* agreement.' That hard bite was back again, sending trepidation dancing along her nerve ends. 'He didn't hold out his end of the deal.'

'Regardless of that, do you have to rub his nose in it like this?' she countered.

'As I said before, I'm a businessman, *anjo*. And I currently have a yacht worth tens of millions of dollars that needs an owner. The Boat Show starts next week. I relocated aboard in order to get it in shape for prospective buyers, otherwise our dinner would have taken place at my residence in Leblon and your brother's delicate feelings would've been spared.'

She frowned. 'You're selling the boat?' The thought of the beautiful vessel going to some unknown, probably pompous new owner made her nose wrinkle in distaste. The design was exquisite, unique…sort of like its owner.

As hard as she tried to imagine it, she couldn't see anyone else owning the boat besides Theo. Not even Pietro. Its black and gold contrasts depicted darkness and light in a complementary synergy—two fascinating characteristics she'd glimpsed more than once in Theo.

'Needs must.'

She looked around the beautiful deck, imagined its graceful lines awash with sunlight, and sighed.

Theo's eyes narrowed as he stared across at her. 'You like the boat.'

'Yes, it's…beautiful.'

He watched her for a few minutes then he nodded. 'Let's make a date for Sunday afternoon. We'll take her out for a quick spin.'

She laughed. 'Unless I'm mistaken, this is a four hundred foot vessel. You don't just take her out for a *quick* spin.'

'A long spin, then. I need to make sure it runs perfectly. If you still like it when we return to shore, I'll keep it.'

Her heart lurched then sped up like a runaway freight train. 'You would do that…for me?'

'*Sim*,' he replied simply.

Genuine puzzlement, along with a heavy dose of excitement she didn't want to admit to, made her blurt, 'Why?'

He strolled lazily to where she stood. This close, she had to tilt her head to catch his gaze. *Darkness and light.* He might have been smiling but Inez could almost reach out and touch the undercurrent of emotions swirling beneath his civility. She jumped slightly when he brushed a forefinger down her cheek.

'Because I intend to keep you, *anjo.* And while you will not have a lot of choice in the matter, I'm willing to make a few adjustments to ensure your contentment.'

CHAPTER FIVE

THEO WATCHED HER grapple with what he'd just said. Unlike her brother, she wasn't inebriated—she'd barely touched her glass of the rich Barolo 2009 he'd specially chosen for their dinner.

She shook her head in confusion. 'You intend to *keep* me?'

Her skin, satin-smooth beneath his touch, begged to be caressed. He gave in to the urge and traced her from cheek to jaw. When she withdrew from him, he followed. He stroked the pulse beating in her neck and pushed back the need to step closer, touch his mouth to the spot.

He'd learnt two things last night.

The first was that Benedicto da Costa, for all his cunning and veneer of sophistication, was still a greedy, vicious snake who thought he could con millions of dollars out of an unsuspecting fool like him.

The second was that Inez da Costa could be a key player in the slow and painful revenge he intended to exact for the wrong done to him. It didn't hurt that the chemistry between them burned the very air they breathed.

In the past Theo had made several opportune decisions by switching tactics at the last minute and making the most of whatever situation he found himself him.

With the newfound information at his fingertips, he'd found a way not only to end the da Costas once and for all, but also to make a tidy profit to boot.

He barely stopped himself from smiling as he looked down into Inez's face. She really was stunningly beautiful. With a mouth that begged to be explored.

'Mr Pantelides?'

'Theo,' he murmured, anticipating her refusal to use his first name.

She blew out an exasperated breath. 'Theo. Explain yourself.'

The unexpected sound of his name on her lips sent a pulse of heat through his body. Followed swiftly by a feeling he recognised as pleasure.

With a silent curse he dropped his hand. Pleasure featured nowhere on his mission to Rio. Nor was standing around, gazing into the face that reminded him of the painting of an angel that used to hang in his father's house.

Pain. Reparation. Merciless humiliation. Those were his objectives.

'There's no hidden message in there, *anjo*. For the duration of my stay in Rio I expect you to make yourself available to me, day and night.'

Her genuine laughter echoed around the open deck. When he didn't join in, she quickly sobered. 'Oh, I'm sorry. But I believe you have me confused with a certain type of woman you must encounter on your travels.'

Theo let the insult slide. He'd told his skipper to take his time with the tour, but even his trusted employee couldn't keep Pietro away for ever. And it looked as if he needed to step up this part of his strategy in order to forward his overall objective.

'I was supposed to sign documents that guaranteed your father's campaign funds this morning but I didn't turn up. Aren't you even a little bit curious as to why?'

A touch of confusion clouded her brown eyes but she shrugged one silky-smooth shoulder that shimmered softly under the deck lights. 'Your business with my father is not my concern.'

A little of that control he kept under a tight leash threatened to slip free. 'You don't care where the money comes from as long as you're kept in the style to which you've grown accustomed, is that it?'

Her eyes widened at the acid leaching from his tone. 'You may think you know me but, I assure you, you've got things wrong—'

'Have I? From where I'm standing it's very evident you're the bait he uses to trap weak, pathetic fools into opening their wallets.'

Her ragged gasp accompanied a look of outrage so near authentic Theo would've believed her reaction had he not seen her in action with Delgado last night.

'If it is your intention to be offensive to show your *machismo*, then *bravo*, you've succeeded,' she threw at him and whirled away.

He caught her wrist before she could take a step.

'Let me go.'

'I've yet to outline my plans, *anjo*.'

'I think you've *outlined* enough. I won't stand here listening to your unfounded insults. I'm going to find Pietro. And then we're leaving.' She tried to free herself. He tightened his grip until he could feel her pulse under his fingers. Furious. Passionate.

His groin stirred and he forced himself to ignore the throb of arousal determined to make itself known. 'You're not leaving here until we have this discussion.'

'What we're having is not a discussion, *senhor*. What you're doing is holding me captive, torturing me with—'

She broke off, no doubt in reaction to his hiss of fury and the flash of icy memory that made his whole body go rigid for one long second.

Theo released her, turned away sharply and shoved his hand through his hair. He noted his fingers' faint trembling and willed himself to stop shaking.

'Th…Theo?' Her voice came from far away, filled with confusion and a touch of concern.

He willed away the effect of the trigger words and forced himself to breathe. But they pounded through his brain nonetheless—*captive, prisoner, torture, darkness…*

Fingers closed over his shoulder and he jerked around. *'Don't!'*

She jumped back, snatching back her hand. It took several more seconds for him to recall where he was. He wasn't in some deep, dark hole in a remote farm in Spain. He was in Rio. With the daughter of the man who continued to cause his recurring nightmares.

'What's…what's wrong with you?' she asked with a wary frown.

He drew in a steady breath and gritted his teeth. 'Nothing. I'll get to the point. The agreement was that I'd take control of Da Costa Holdings and keep a fifty per cent share of the profits in exchange for liquidated funds to finance your father's political campaign. However, the papers your father had drawn up contain a major loophole that I can easily exploit.'

Slowly, his panic receded and he noticed she was absently rubbing her wrist. He quickly replayed his reaction to her touch and breathed a sigh of relief when he confirmed to himself that he hadn't grabbed her in his panic.

She continued to rub her skin and slowly another earthy emotion replaced his roiling feelings. He welcomed the pulse of arousal despite the fact that he had no intention of falling prey to the easy wiles of Inez da Costa. No matter how mouth-watering her body or how angelic her face.

'Shouldn't you be telling my father this, give him a chance to fix the loophole before you sign?'

He smiled at her naiveté. 'Why should I? I stand to gain by signing the agreement as it's drawn up.'

Her brow creased. 'Then why tell me about it? What's

to keep me from telling my father about it the moment I leave here?'

'You won't.'

One expertly plucked eyebrow lifted. 'Again, I think you underestimate me.'

He strode to the extensively stocked bar and poured himself a shot of vodka. 'You won't because if you do I won't sign the agreement in any form. And the offer of financial backing vanishes.'

All trace of colour left her face. 'So this is a blackmail attempt. To what purpose?'

'The purpose needn't concern you. All I want you to know is that there is a loophole which I can choose to exploit or leave alone, depending on your cooperation.'

'But what is to stop you from going ahead with whatever you have planned after I've cooperated with…what exactly is it you want from me?'

'That's the simple part, *anjo*. I want to keep you. Until such time as I tire of you. Then you will be set free.'

When the full meaning of his words finally became clear, ice cascaded down Inez's spine. Despite the warm temperature, she shivered.

Oh, how easily he said the words. As if her answer meant nothing to him. But of course it did. He'd been planning this for a while. The meeting this morning outside the coffee shop—which she was now certain hadn't been coincidental—the dinner invitation that he'd probably known her father wouldn't be able to attend due to his long-standing monthly dinner with the oil minister, the invitation to the yacht, which was sure to cause a reaction in her brother, letting Pietro drink far more than he should've so he'd get her alone…

'You planned this,' she accused in a hushed tone because her throat was working to swallow down her rising anger.

'I plan everything, Inez,' he replied simply.

She looked into his face. The indomitable determination stamped on his harsh features sent a wave of anxiety through her.

She started to speak, to say the words that seemed unreal to her and her mouth trembled. His gaze dropped to the telling reaction and she immediately clamped her lips together. Showing weakness would only get her eaten alive.

Not that she wouldn't be anyway. A bubble of hysteria threatened. She swallowed and held his gaze.

'You want me to be your *mistress*?'

He laughed long and deeply. 'Is that what you would call yourself?'

She flushed. 'How else would you describe what you've just demanded of me? This *keeping* me? What you're suggesting is archaic enough to be described as such. Or does *plaything* more suit your pseudo-modernistic outlook?'

'No, Inez. I don't like the term plaything either. I have no intention of playing with you. No, what I foresee for us is much more grown up than that.' The sexual intent behind the statement was unmistakable.

Rather than being offended or shocked, Inez found herself growing breathless. Excited.

No!

'Yes,' he murmured as if he'd read her mind.

'Whatever term you slap on your intentions, I refuse to be a part of it. I'm going to find my brother—'

He slowly sank onto the plush seat, curved his hand along the back of the chair and levelled one ankle over his knee. 'And tell him that you've dashed his hopes of a possible high profile position in your father's administration because you couldn't take one for the team? I don't think you're in a position to refuse any demands I make, *anjo*.'

'Stop calling me that! And I won't be a pawn in whatever game you're playing with my father and brother. Pietro is well aware of that.'

'Really? Since when? Wasn't serving on your father's

campaign the reason you dropped out of university? Clearly, you play a part in your father's political ambitions or you wouldn't have been trying to fleece poor Alfonso. Why stop now when you're so close to achieving your goals? And why claim innocence when it's something you've done before?'

The hurt that scythed through her was deep and jagged. She wasn't aware she'd moved until she stood over him, glaring down at the arrogant face that wore that oh, so self-assured smile.

'I've never wanted to be this…this person you think I am. I was merely trying to help my family. I misjudged the situation and—'

'You mean you fell in love with your mark.'

She swallowed. 'I don't know what you're getting at.' But deep down she suspected.

'I mean you were set a target and you fell in love with your target. Isn't that what happened with Blanco?'

Light-headedness assailed her as he confirmed her suspicion. 'You know about Constantine?'

'I know everything I need to know about your family, *anjo*. But by all means enlighten me as to why you've been so misjudged.'

His cynicism raked her nerves raw. 'I made a mistake, one that I freely admit to.'

'What mistake do you mean, *querida*? I want to hear it.'

'I misjudged a man I thought I could trust.'

'You mean you meant to use him but found out he intended to use you too?' he mocked. 'Some would call that poetic justice.'

Recalling Constantine's public humiliation of her, the names he'd called her in the press, her stomach turned over. 'You're despicable.' She raised her chin. 'And assuming you're even close to being right, won't I be a fool to repeat that mistake again?'

'No.'

'No?'

His eyes fixed on hers. Serious and intense. 'Because this time you know exactly what you're getting. There will be no delusions of love on either of our parts. No pretence. Just a task, executed with smooth efficiency.'

'But you intend to parade me about as your…lover? What will everyone think?'

He shrugged. 'I don't care what everyone thinks. And I don't much think that bothers you either.'

She shivered. 'Of course it bothers me. What makes you think it won't?'

'You're the ultimate young Rio socialite. You have a dedicated following and young impressionable girls can't wait to grow up and be you.' His mockery was unmistakable.

Heat crept up her cheeks. 'That's just the media spinning itself out of control.'

'Carefully fuelled by you to help your father's status. You're always seen with the right offspring of the right ministers and CEOs. You're the attraction to draw the young voters, are you not?'

She couldn't deny the allegation because it was true. Nor did she want to waste time straying away from the more serious subject of the demand he was making of her.

The demand she wouldn't—*couldn't*—consent to.

But there was something about him…a reassurance… and expectation of acquiescence that made the hairs on her nape stand on end.

'What happens if I refuse this…this sleazy proposal?'

'I sign the agreement then use the company as I wish. I could dismantle it piece by piece and sell it off for a neat profit. Or I could just drive down the share price and watch the company implode from the inside out. But that's all boring business. What do you care?'

Her fists clenched. 'I care because my grandfather built that company from nothing.'

'And now your father's willing to hand it over to a complete stranger just so he can further his political career.'

She pursed her lips and fought not to react. She'd been deeply concerned when she'd first heard how her father planned to raise funds for his campaign. Concerns that had been airily brushed away with reassurances of airtight clauses.

Clauses which Theo had apparently easily loopholed.

Maybe it wasn't too late. She could tell him to go to hell and warn her father and brother about the danger their proposed business partner presented and advise them to walk away. Surely that would be better than admitting the lion into their midst and letting him wreak havoc at whim?

Light hazel eyes watched her with a predatory gleam. 'If you're thinking of warning your family, I'd think twice. Remember how easily I dispatched Delgado?'

She stiffened, recalling how a few whispered words had caused one investor in her father's campaign to walk away. 'You don't mean that,' she tried.

He slowly rose from the chair and towered over her. Every protective instinct screamed at her to step back but she stood her ground. Any show of weakness would be mercilessly pounced on.

'Do you want to test me, *anjo*?' The blade of steel that hovered over the endearment sent a shiver down her spine.

She slowly uncurled her fists and forced herself to breathe. 'What do you expect me to do?'

His smile was equally as predatory as the look in his eyes. 'You will inform your father and brother tomorrow that you and I are an item—our meeting last night sparked a chemistry so hot we couldn't *not* be together.'

A tiny sliver of relief eased her constricted chest. 'If that's all you want, I'm sure I can convince them—'

His mocking smile stopped her words.

'After you tell them that, you'll pack your bags and move in with me.'

Shock slammed her sideways. 'Are you serious?'

He gripped her chin and held her pinned under his gaze. 'I've never been more serious in my life.'

'But…why?'

'My reasons are my own. You just need to do as you're told.'

Do as you're told. Constantine had tried to blackmail her with those very words. When she'd refused he'd spread rumours about her in the newspapers.

Anger grew in her belly. But it was a helpless anger born of the knowledge that there was nothing she could do. Once again she was trapped in a hell that came from trying to do what was right for her family.

Only this time she was to truly pay with her body. In a stranger's bed. Her heart tripped before going into fierce overdrive.

She gazed at Theo's face, then his body. A body she would in the very near future become scorchingly intimate with. The horror she'd expected to feel oddly did not materialise.

'How long exactly will I be expected to *do as I'm told*?' she snapped.

'Until after the elections.'

A horrified gasp escaped her throat and she forcibly wrenched herself from his grip. 'But…that's…the elections are *three months* away!'

'*Sim*,' he replied simply.

'*Sim*? You expect me to put my life on hold for the next three months, just like that?' She clicked her fingers.

He raised an eyebrow. 'Do you want me to repeat the part about you not having a choice?'

She searched his face, trying to find meaning behind his intentions. 'What did my father do? Did he best you at a deal? Bad-mouth you to investors? Because I can't see what would make you want to go down this path of trying to get your own back.'

She watched his eyes darken, and his nostrils flare. All

traces of mockery were wiped from his face as he stared down at her. Only she was sure he wasn't really seeing her.

His usual intense focus dulled for several seconds and his jaw clenched so tight she feared it could crack. Whatever memory he was reliving caused volcanic fury to bubble beneath the harsh, ragged breath he expelled and this time she did take that step back, purely for self-preservation.

Voices sounded on the deck below. In a few minutes Pietro and the skipper would return from their tour. Inez wasn't sure whether to be grateful for the disruption or frustrated that her opportunity to find out Theo's reasons for demanding her presence in his bed had been thwarted.

His gaze sharpened, flicked towards the steps and back to her.

'It's time for your answer. Do you agree to my terms?'

She shook her head. 'Not until you tell me— *what are you doing*?' she blurted as he snapped out an arm and tugged her close.

One large bold hand gripped her waist and the other speared through her hair. Completely captured, she couldn't move as he angled her face to his. The unsettling fury was still evident in his darkened eyes and taut mouth. Despite the heat transmitted from his grip, she shivered.

'You seem to think you can talk or question your way out of this, *anjo*. You can't. But perhaps it was a mistake to expect a verbal agreement. Perhaps a physical demonstration is what's best?'

Despite his rhetorical question, she tried to answer. 'No…'

'Yes!' he muttered fiercely. Then his mouth smashed down on hers.

She'd been kissed before. By casual boyfriends in her late teens who she'd felt safe enough with.

By Constantine, in the beginning, before he'd revealed his true ruthless colours.

Nothing of what had gone before prepared her for the power and expertise behind Theo's kiss. Her world tilted beneath her feet as his tongue ruthlessly breached the seam of her lips. Hot, erotically charged and savagely determined, he invaded her mouth with searing passion. Bold and brazen, he flicked his tongue against hers, tasting her once and coming back for more.

The shocked little noise she made was a cross between surprise and her body's stunned reaction to the invasion.

The hand at her waist pressed her closer to his body. Whipcord strength, sleek muscles and his own unique scent brought different sensations that attacked her flailing senses.

Fire lashed through her belly as liquid heat pooled between her thighs. Her breasts, crushed against his chest, swelled and ached, her nipples peaking into demanding points with a swiftness that made her dizzy.

Deus!

Feeling her world career even faster out of control, she threw up her hands. Hard muscle rippled beneath her fingers. The need to explore slammed into her. Before she could question her actions, she slid her hands over his warm cotton-covered shoulders to his nape, her fingers tingling as they encountered his bare skin.

He jerked beneath her touch, pulled back with a tug on her hair. Breathing harshly, he stared into her eyes for several seconds. Hunger blazed in his, turning them a dark, mesmerising molten gold that stole what little breath she had from her lungs. Then his eyes dropped lower to her parted mouth.

A rough sound rumbled from his throat. Then he was kissing her again. Harder, more demanding, more possessively than before.

Inez pushed her fingers through his hair as arousal like she'd never experienced before bit deep. This time, when his tongue slid into her mouth, she met it with hers. Boldly, she tried to give as much as she got, although she knew she was hopelessly inadequate when it came to experience.

The hand around her waist tightened and she was lifted off her feet. Seconds later, she found herself on the bar stool, her legs splayed and Theo firmly between thighs exposed by her stance. He came at her again, the force of his sensual attack tilting the stool backwards.

She threw out her hands onto the counter to keep from toppling over. Theo growled beneath his breath, his hands moving upward from her waist to cup her breasts. He moulded her willing, aching flesh so expertly she whimpered and arched into his hold. Beneath her clothes, her tight nipples unfurled in eager anticipation when his thumbs grazed over them. The deep pleasurable shudder made him repeat the action, eliciting a soft cry of pleasure from deep inside her.

'Inez!'

The rapier-sharp call of her name doused her with ice-cold water. She wrenched herself from Theo's hold...or at least she tried to.

The hands that had dropped from her breasts to her waist at the sound of Pietro's return stayed her desperate flight.

'What the *hell* do you think you're doing?' Pietro growled, no longer looking as drunk as he'd been half an hour ago.

'If you need it explained to you, da Costa, then I'm wondering who the hell I'm getting into business with.'

Her brother flushed in anger. 'I wasn't talking to you, Pantelides. But maybe I should ask you what you're doing, pawing my sister like some mad animal.'

Inez desperately tried to pull her dress down. But Theo stood firmly between her thighs, making the task impossible. Her sound of distress drew his attention from Pietro. He stared down at her for a second before he adjusted his stance. But although he allowed her to close her legs and pull her dress down, his hands didn't drop from her waist.

If anything, they tightened, their hold so possessive she fought to breathe.

'Inez was going to tell you tomorrow. But I guess tonight's as good a time as any.'

Pietro's gaze shifted from Theo's face to hers. 'Tell me what?'

'Do you want to do the honours, *anjo*? Or shall I?' he queried softly.

Her heartbeat accelerated but not with the arousal pounding through her bloodstream. She heard the clear warning in Theo's tone. Anything short of what he'd demanded of her would see her family ruined completely.

She opened her mouth. Closed it again and swallowed hard.

A trace of fear washed over Pietro's face. Despite their strained relationship, there'd been times in the past when they'd been close. She knew how much a political career of his own some day meant to him. How much he was pinning his hopes on what her father's campaign would mean to him personally.

She tried again to speak the words Theo demanded she speak. But her vocal cords wouldn't work.

'Would someone hurry up and tell me what's going on?'

Fierce hazel eyes drifted over her face in a look that spelled possession so potent her breath caught.

Theo curled his arm over her shoulders and pulled her into the heat of his body. He drifted his mouth over her temple in an adoring move so utterly convincing she reeled at his skilful deception.

She was grappling with that, and with just how much of the kiss they'd shared had been an exercise in pure ruthless seduction on his part, when he spoke.

'Your sister and I have become…enamoured with each other. We only met last night but already I cannot bear to be without her.' His voice held none of the mockery from before, sparking another stunned realisation of his skill. He stared down at her and she caught the implacable determination in his eyes.

When his gaze reconnected with Pietro's she stared, mesmerised, at his profile then shivered at the iron-hard set to his jaw.

'Tomorrow she will be moving out of your home. And into mine.'

CHAPTER SIX

'*LIKE HELL YOU are*,' Pietro repeated for the hundredth time as their chauffeur-driven car stopped outside the opulent Ipanema mansion she'd grown up in.

She quickly threw open the door and hurried up the steps leading to the double oak front doors although she knew escape wouldn't be easy. Pietro was hard on her heels.

'Did you hear what I said?' he demanded.

'I heard you loud and clear. But you fail to realise I'm no longer a child. I'm twenty-four years old—well over the age when I can do whatever the heck I want.'

He slid a hand through his hair. 'Look, I know I may have pushed you into playing a greater part in *Pai*'s fund-raising campaign. But…I don't think getting involved with Pantelides is a good idea,' he said abruptly.

Inez's heart lurched at his concern but she couldn't re-assure him because she herself didn't know what the future held. 'Thank you for your concern but like I said, I'm a grown up.'

He swivelled on his heel in the vast entrance hall of the villa. 'Are you really that into him? I know what I saw on his deck tells its own story but you only met him last night!'

'I hadn't met Alfonso Delgado before last night either and yet you expected me to charm him.'

'*Charm* him, not move in with him!'

'There's no point arguing with me. My mind is made up.'

Pietro's face darkened. 'Is this some sort of rebellion?'

Inez sighed. 'Of course not. But I'd planned to move out anyway, once you and *Pai* started on the campaign trail.'

'Move out and go where? This is your home, Inez,' he replied.

She shook her head. 'My world doesn't begin and end in this house, Pietro. I intend to rent an apartment, get a job.'

'Then don't start by ruining yourself with Pantelides.'

Her throat clogged. 'My reputation is already in shreds after Constantine. I really have nothing left to lose.'

She turned to head up the grand staircase that led to the twin wings of their villa. Behind her, she could still hear Pietro pacing the hallway.

'This doesn't make any sense, Inez. Perhaps a good night's sleep will bring you to your senses.'

She didn't answer. Because she didn't want to waste her time telling him the decision had already been made for her.

For Theo to have gone to the effort of staging that kiss and paving the way for the lies she had to perpetuate, she knew without a shadow of a doubt that his demands were real.

He'd gone to a lot of trouble to set up tonight's meeting. She would be a fool to bait him to see if he would carry out his threat.

Her heart hammered as she undressed and stepped beneath the shower. Slowly soaping her body, she found her mind drifting back to their kiss. The incandescent delirium of it was unlike anything she'd felt before.

Her fingers touched her lips, and they tingled in remembrance.

Tomorrow she was inviting herself into the lion's den to be devoured whole for the sake of her family.

A hysterical laugh became lost in the sound of the running water.

Pietro was finally showing signs of being the brother she remembered before their mother died. Shame that she'd had to sacrifice herself on the altar of their family's prosperity before he'd come round. As for her father…sadness engulfed her at the thought that even if he knew of her sacrifice, he probably wouldn't lift a finger to shield her from it.

Theo's gaze strayed to his phone for the umpteenth time in under twenty minutes and he cursed under his breath.

He'd called Inez this morning and they'd agreed a time of eleven o'clock, two hours before he was due to sign the documents at her father's office.

It was now eleven twenty-five and there was no sign of her. No big deal. She was probably stuck in traffic. Or she hadn't left her home on time, especially if she was packing for a three-month stay.

Besides, women are always late.

Even as a child he'd known this. His mother had never been on time for a single event in her life.

His mother…

Memory rained down vicious blows that had him catching his breath. His mother, the woman who'd been nowhere in sight, either before or after he was kidnapped and held for ransom by Benedicto da Costa's vicious thugs.

For weeks after he'd been rescued and returned home, broken and devastated by his ordeal, he'd asked for his mother. Ari had made several excuses for her absence. But Theo had been unable to reconcile the fact that the mother who'd once treated him as if he'd been the centre of her world suddenly couldn't even be bothered to pick up the phone and enquire about her mentally and physically traumatised child.

No. She'd been too preoccupied with wallowing in her misery following her husband's betrayal to bother with her own children.

Ari had been the one to hold them together after their family was shattered by the press uncovering their father's many shady dealings and philandering ways.

For a very long time he'd laboured under the misconception that out of the three brothers he was the most special in their father's eyes. That just because he was the miracle baby his parents had never thought they'd have, he was their favourite. His kidnapping and what he'd uncovered since had mercilessly ripped that indulgent blindfold away.

Finding out that his father had known about Benedicto da Costa's escalating threats and that he'd done nothing to warn or protect him had forced the cruellest reality on him.

And his mother's response to all that had been to abandon him, together with her other two children, and go into hiding.

Hearing of his father's eventual death had made him even angrier at being robbed of the chance to look his father in the eye and see the monster for himself.

Because, even now, a pathetic part of him clung to the hope that maybe his father hadn't known the full extent of the kidnapping threat; hadn't known that Benedicto da Costa's reaction to being thwarted out of a business deal would be to kidnap a seventeen-year-old boy, and have his torture photographed and sent to his family to pressure them into finding the millions of dollars owed to him.

His phone rang, wrenching him out of the bitter recollections. Glancing down at the number, a bolt of white-hot anger lanced through him. He forced himself to wait for a couple more rings before he answered it. 'Pantelides.'

'*Bom dia.* I've just had a very interesting conversation with my daughter.' Theo detected the throb of anger in Benedicto da Costa's voice and a grim smile curved his own lips. 'She seems determined to pursue this rather *sudden* course of action where you're concerned.'

'Your daughter strikes me as a very determined woman who knows exactly what she wants,' he replied smoothly.

'She is. All the same, I can't help think that this decision is rather precipitate.' There was clear suspicion in Benedicto's voice now.

'Trust me, it's been very well thought through on my part. Tell me, Benedicto, has she left yet?'

'*Sim*, against my wishes, she has left home,' he replied, his voice taut with displeasure.

A wave of satisfaction swept through Theo. 'Good. I'll await her arrival.'

'I hope this will not delay our meeting,' the older man enquired.

'Don't worry. The moment I welcome your daughter into my home, I'll head to your offices.'

An edgy silence greeted his answer and Theo could sense him weighing his words to perceive a possible threat. Finally, Benedicto answered, 'We should celebrate our partnership once the documents are signed.'

Theo's mouth twisted. Benedicto had already moved on from the subject of his daughter. And he noticed there had been no admonition to treat her well, *or else...*

But the knowledge that Benedicto had intensely disapproved of Inez's intentions and had called him to air that disapproval was good enough for him.

'Great idea. Unfortunately, I'll be busy for the next few nights. Perhaps some time next week Inez and I will have you and Pietro over for dinner.'

The fiery exhalation that greeted his indelicate words made Theo's grin widen.

'Of course. I'll look forward to it. *Até a próxima,*' Benedicto said tightly.

Theo ended the call without responding. He absorbed the pulse of triumph rushing through his bloodstream for a pleasurable second before he exhaled.

His plan was far from being executed. But this was a brilliant start.

He looked out of the floor to ceiling window at the sparkling pool and the beach beyond and tried to push away the images that had visited him again last night and the single hoarse scream that had woken him.

A full body shudder raked his frame and he shoved a hand through his hair. Although he'd long ago accepted the nightmares as part of his existence, he loathed their presence and the helplessness he felt in those endless moments when he was caught in their grip.

The single therapy session he'd let Ari talk him into attending had mentioned triggers and the importance of anxiety-detectors.

He laughed under his breath. Putting himself within touching distance of the man responsible for those nightmares would be termed as foolhardy by most definitions.

Theo chose to believe that exacting excruciating revenge would heal him. *An eye for an eye.*

And if he had to suffer a few side-effects during the process, then so be it.

He tensed as his security intercom buzzed. Crossing the vast sun-dappled room, he picked up the handset.

'*Senhor*, there's a Senhorita da Costa here to see you.'

A throb of a different nature invaded his bloodstream. 'Let her in,' he instructed.

Replacing the handset, he found himself striding to the front door and out onto his driveway before he realised what he was doing.

Hands on his hips, he watched her tiny green sports car appear on his long driveway. The top was down and the wind was blowing through her loose thick hair. Stylish sunglasses shielded her eyes from him but he knew she was watching him just as he was studying her.

She brought the car to a smooth stop a few feet from him and turned off the ignition. For several seconds the only sound that impinged on the late morning air was the water cascading from the stone nymph's urn into the fountain bowl. Then the sound of her seat belt retracting joined the tinkling.

'You're late,' he breathed.

She pulled out her keys and opened her door. 'It took

a while to uproot myself from the only home I've ever known,' she said waspishly.

A touch from a well-manicured finger and the boot popped open. He strolled forward, viewed its contents and his eyes narrowed.

'And yet you only packed two suitcases for a three-month stay?' he remarked darkly. 'I hope you don't think you can run back to *Pai*'s house each time you need a new toothbrush?'

She got out of the car.

From across the width of the open top, she glared at him. 'I can afford to buy my own toothbrush, thanks,' she retorted.

Theo nodded. 'Good to hear it.' Unable to stop himself, his gaze travelled down her body.

Faded jeans moulded her hips and her cream scooped-neck silk top left her arms bare. Its short-in-the-front, longer-at-the-back design exposed a delicious inch of golden, smooth midriff when she turned to shut her door and the air lifted the light material.

Heat invaded his groin, once again reminding him of their kiss last night.

The kiss that had blown him clean away and rendered him almost incoherent by the time her brother had rudely interrupted them.

Hell, she'd been so responsive, so intoxicatingly passionate, she'd gone to his head within seconds. What had set out as a hammering-a-point-home exercise to convince her he meant business had swiftly morphed into something else. Something he'd still been struggling to decipher when she'd been hustled off his boat by her suddenly protective brother.

One thing he'd been certain of was that had Pietro been a few more minutes returning to the top deck, Theo was sure he would've had his hands on her bare skin, exploring her in a more earthy way, propriety be damned.

Luckily, he'd come to his senses. And, from here on in, he intended to focus on his plan and his plan alone.

She went to the boot and bent over to lift the first case. The sight of her rounded bottom made a vein throb in his temple.

He stepped forward, grabbed the cases from her and handed them to his hovering butler. 'I'm running late for my meeting. We should have done this last night like I suggested.'

He'd tried. But she'd stood her ground and he had quickly decided that there was nothing to be gained from getting into a slanging match with Pietro da Costa. That he'd also realised that his change of timing was to do with that kiss and nothing to do with his carefully laid plans had had him sharply reassessing his priorities.

'I'm here now. Don't let me stop you from leaving if you wish to.'

He smiled at the undisguised hope in her voice. 'Now what kind of host would I be if I desert you the moment you turn up?'

'The same as the one who blackmailed me into this situation in the first place?' she replied caustically.

There was a thread of unhappiness in her voice that grated at him.

'This will go a lot easier if you accept the status quo.'

'You mean just shut up and *do as I'm told*?' she snapped bitterly as she slammed the boot shut and walked towards him.

Unease weaved through him. With restless shoulders, he shrugged it away. 'No. You can protest all you want. I just want you to be aware of the futility of it.'

She snorted under her breath, a sound that made his smile widen. She had spirit, and wasn't afraid to bare her claws when cornered. Which made him wonder why she withstood the unreasonable control from her father. Were material benefits so important to her?

The heavy glass front door slid shut behind them and he watched her reaction to his house. It was an architectural masterpiece, and had featured in several top magazines before he'd bought it a year ago and ceased all publicity of the award-winning design.

'Wow,' she breathed. 'This place must have cost you a bomb.'

Theo had his answer. Disappointment scythed through him as he watched her move to the bronze sculpture he'd acquired several weeks back.

'I saw the exhibition on this two months ago. This piece is worth a cool half million,' she gasped in wonder. 'And that one—' she pointed to another smaller sculpture he'd commissioned by his favourite New York artist '—is an exclusive piece, worth over two million dollars.'

His lips twisted. 'Should I be worried that you know the monetary value of every piece of art in my house?'

She whirled to face him. 'Excuse me?'

'I hope we can engage in more meaningful dialogue than how much everything is worth. I find the subject of avarice…distasteful.'

Her gasp sounded genuinely hurt-filled. 'I wasn't…I'm just…that's a horrible thing to say, Mr Pantelides.'

His eyebrow lifted. 'I thought I kissed all the formality out of you last night?'

She flushed a delicate pink that made her skin glow. Her expressive brown eyes slid from his and she turned back to examine the room.

It was then that he noticed the faint bruises on her left arm. He was striding to her and lifting her arm to examine the marks before his brain had connected with his body.

'Who did this to you?' he demanded.

Her surprised gaze snapped from his to her arm. Her flush deepened as she swiftly shook her head. 'I…it doesn't matter; it's nothing—'

He swallowed hard. 'Like hell it is.' The idea that his demands on her might have caused this to happen to her made a thread of revulsion rise in his belly. He forced it down and concentrated on her face. 'Tell me who it was.'

She swallowed. 'My father.'

Pure fury blurred his vision for several seconds. 'Your *father* did this to you?'

She gave a jerky nod.

Why the hell was he surprised? 'Has he done anything like this before?' he bit out.

She pressed her lips together in a vain attempt not to answer. A firm grip of her chin, tilting it to his gaze, convinced her otherwise. 'Once. Maybe twice.'

His vicious curse made her shiver. Theo examined the marks, which would grow yellowish by nightfall, and pushed down the mounting fury. 'That son of a bitch will never touch you again.'

Shock made her gasp. 'That *son of a bitch* is my *father*. And I've given you what you wanted, so I expect you to hold up your end of the bargain.'

He frowned with genuine puzzlement. 'Why do you tolerate this, Inez?' He glanced from the bruises to her face. 'You're more than old enough to live on your own. Hell, if money and a rich lifestyle are what you crave, you're sufficiently resourceful to find some wealthy guy who would—'

She snatched her arm from his grasp. It was then that he realised he'd been caressing her soft skin with his thumb. He missed the connection almost immediately.

'I certainly hope you're not about to suggest what I think you are?'

Keen frustration rocked him into movement. 'I'm curious, that's all.'

'I'm not here to satisfy your curiosity. And perhaps you've been lucky enough to be granted a perfect family but not everyone has been afforded the same luxury. We made do with what we... Did I say something funny?' she snapped.

He cut off the mirthless laughter that had bubbled up at

her words. 'Yes. *You're damned hilarious*. You obviously don't know what you're talking about.'

She stared at him with confusion and a little trepidation. 'No. But how can I? We only met two nights ago. And now I'm here, your possession for the foreseeable future.'

The simple statement twisted like live electricity between them. The look in her eyes said she was daring him to react to it. But the off-kilter emotions swirling through his chest made him back away from it. He shouldn't have dealt with her so soon after speaking to Benedicto. He should've left Teresa, his housekeeper, to see to her needs.

He turned and headed for the door. 'I'll show you up-stairs. And then I need to go.'

Striding into the hallway, he started up the grand central stairs that led to the upper two floors of his house. After a few steps, he noticed she wasn't behind him.

Turning, he found her paused on the second step, her gaze once again wide and wondrous as she stared around her.

'What?'

'There are no concrete walls.' She looked up at the all-encompassing glass around her. 'Or ceilings.'

He resumed climbing the stairs. 'I don't like walls. And I don't like ceilings,' he threw over his shoulder.

She hurried after him and caught up with him as they neared the first suite of rooms. She regarded him for a few seconds then bit her lip.

He paused with a hand on the doorknob. 'What?' he asked again, trying and not succeeding in prising his gaze from her plump lips.

'I'm not sure whether to take that as a metaphor or not.'

'*Anjo*, there's no hidden meaning behind my words. I literally do not like concrete walls or ceilings.'

She frowned in puzzlement. 'I don't understand.'

'It's very simple. I don't like being closed in.'

'You're…*claustrophobic*?' She whispered the word as if she wasn't sure how to apply it to him.

He shrugged and hurriedly threw open the door, a part of him reeling at what he'd just admitted. 'We all have our flaws,' he retorted.

'Were you born with it?'

His jaw clenched once. 'No. It was a condition thrust upon me quite against my will.'

'But…you seem…'

'Invincible?' he mocked.

Her lips pursed. 'I was going to say self-assured.'

'Appearances can be deceptive, *querida*. After you.' He indicated the door he'd just opened.

She stopped dead in the middle of the room. From where he stood, Theo could see what she was seeing. With the glass walls and white carpet and furnishings and nothing but the view of the blue sky and sea beyond, the vista was breathtaking.

'*Deus*, I feel as if I'm floating on a cloud,' she murmured with an awe-filled voice.

'That is the primary aim of the property. Light, air, no constrictions.'

He'd learned to his cost that constrictions triggered his anxiety and fuelled his nightmares. Which was why every single property he owned was filled with light.

'It's beautiful.'

The strong pulse of pleasure that washed through him had him stepping back. Things were getting out of hand. He needed to walk away, go to his meeting with Benedicto and remind himself why he was in Rio. This need to bask in Inez's presence, touch her skin, indulge in the urge to taste her sensual lips once more needed to killed. He had to stick to his game plan.

'Make yourself at home. I'll be back later. We're going out this evening. Dinner at Cabana de Ouro, then probably clubbing. Wear something short and sexy.'

Her eyes widened at his curt tone but he was already turning away. He didn't stop until he reached the landing.

On a completely unstoppable urge, he looked over his shoulder. Through the glass walls, he saw her frozen in the middle of her suite, her eyes fixed on him.

She looked lost. And confused. And a little relieved.

With grim determination he turned and headed down the stairs. And he hated himself for needing the reminder that Benedicto da Costa had damaged not just him, but his whole family.

The payback should be equal to the crime committed.

The black satin boy shorts she chose to wear were plenty stylish and sexy. They also moulded her behind much more than she was strictly comfortable with but everything else she'd hastily packed was too formal for dinner at Cabana de Ouro, the trendy restaurant and bar in Ipanema. Coupled with the dark gold silk top, with her hair piled on top of her head and gold hoops in her ears and bangles on her wrist, she looked good enough for whatever club Theo intended to take her to after dinner.

Clubbing wasn't strictly her entertainment of choice. But since, for the next twelve weeks, Theo expected her to obey his every command, the least she could do was learn to pick her battles. And she'd already endured one battle this morning in the form of confrontation with Theo. And found out he was claustrophobic.

He'd been right; she'd secretly imagined him to be invincible. The way he carried himself, the innate authority and self-assurance that seemed part of his genetic make up, she'd had no trouble seeing him best each situation he found himself him.

Hearing him admit to a deep flaw that most grown men would be ashamed of had floored her. Coupled with his concern when he'd seen the marks her father had inflicted when she'd announced she was moving in with Theo, she'd been seriously floundering in a sea of uncertainty by the time he'd left her bedroom.

She examined the marks on her arm now and released a shaky breath to see that they were fading. She was shrugging on the shoulder-padded waist-length leather jacket that went with the outfit when she heard Theo's Aston Martin roar into the driveway.

Her fingers trembled as she fastened the long-chained gold medallion necklace at her nape.

He'd left her so abruptly this morning she hadn't had the time to question him about sleeping arrangements. A closer examination of her suite after he'd left had revealed no presence of another occupant, and after talking to Teresa, his housekeeper, she'd found out that the *senhor*'s suite was directly above hers, taking up the whole glass-roofed top floor of the house.

The fact that she wouldn't be expected to share his bed immediately should've pleased her. Instead she was more on edge than ever. Or maybe that was what he wanted? That she should be kept guessing, kept on a knife-edge of uncertainty like some sort of game?

Deus!

She'd barely spent one day under his glass roof and already she was being driven mad. His response to her admiring his sculptures had been too infuriating for her to explain how she'd come to acquire such knowledge of sculptures—her late mother's talent. If he wanted to believe Inez appreciated beautiful art purely with dollar signs in her eyes, that was his problem.

Her breath caught as she heard distinct footsteps in the hallway. Teresa had shown her how to shroud the bedroom glass for privacy and she'd activated it before she'd gone in to take a shower. It was still shrouded now although she could make out a faint outline of the towering man who knocked a few seconds later.

'Come in.' She cringed at the husky breathlessness of her voice.

The heavy glass swung back and Theo stood framed in the doorway.

Light hazel eyes locked on her with the force of a laser beam for several seconds before they travelled slowly down her body.

Before meeting him, Inez would've found it hard to believe she could physically react so strongly to a look from a man. Constantine, with all his misleading smiles and false charm, had never affected her like this, not even when she'd believed herself in love with him.

With Theo the evidence was irrefutable—in the accelerated beat of her heart, the tightening and heaviness of her breasts and the stinging heat that spread outward from her belly like a flash fire.

She watched his mouth drop open as his gaze reached her shorts and her own mouth dried at the look that settled on his face.

'What the hell are you wearing?'

'What? I'm wearing clothes, Mr Pantelides,' she snapped, once she was able to get her brain working again.

He stepped into the room and the door slid shut behind him. All at once, she became aware of the sheer size of him, of the restriction in her breathing and the fact that her eyes were devouring his magnificent form.

'Let's get one thing straight. From now on you'll address me as Theo. No more *senhor* and no more Mr Pantelides, understand?'

'Is that an order?' She tilted her chin to see his face as he stopped before her.

'It's a friendly warning that there will be consequences if you don't comply.'

'What consequences?' she huffed.

'How about every time you call me *senhor* I kiss that sassy mouth of yours?'

CHAPTER SEVEN

'EXCUSE ME?' HER voice was a little more breathless. With excitement. *Deus*, what was wrong with her? This man was threatening her family, was effectively turning her life upside down for the sake of some unknown grudge. And all she could think of was him kissing her again.

'No, you're not excused. Use my first name or I'll kiss it into you. Your choice. Now tell me what the hell you're wearing.' His gaze dropped back to her shorts, his eyes glazing with hunger so acute, her heart hammered.

'These are shorts. You said "short and sexy".'

His mouth worked for a few seconds before he nodded. 'I said short, but I don't think I meant that short, *anjo*.'

Heat raced up her neck and she barely managed to stop her hand from connecting with his face. 'They are not that bad.'

His rasping laugh made her face flame. 'Trust me, from where I'm standing, they're lethal.'

'I have nothing else to change into. Everything else is too formal for a club.'

Dark eyes rose, almost reluctantly, to clash with hers. 'I find that very hard to believe.'

'It's true. I didn't have enough time to pack properly. Besides, I didn't take you for…'

His eyes narrowed. 'Didn't take me for what?'

She shrugged. 'You don't strike me as the clubbing type.'

One corner of his mouth lifted. 'Have you been forming impressions about me, *anjo*?'

She kicked herself for that revelatory remark. 'Not really.'

He looked down at her shorts one more time and he turned abruptly for the door. 'I'll be ready to go in fifteen minutes. You can tell me what other impressions you've formed about me at dinner.'

Inez exhaled and realised she hadn't taken a full breath since he'd walked into her presence. Her whole body quivered as she shoved her feet into three-inch platforms and made sure her cell phone and lipstick were in the black and gold clutch.

She caught sight of herself in the hallway mirror as she made her way down and cringed at the feverish look in her eyes.

Reassuring herself firmly that it was anger at Theo for his overbearing treatment of her, she made her way to the living room.

Floodlights illuminated the pool and gardens in a stunning display of shimmering light and shrubbery. Like every single aspect of the building, the sight was so breathtaking her fingers itched with the need to draw.

Setting her clutch down, she went to the large duffel bag she'd brought down this afternoon and took out her sketchpad and pencil.

She was so lost in capturing the vista before her, she didn't sense Theo enter the room until his unique scent wrapped itself around her.

She jerked around to see him standing close behind her, his eyes on her picture.

'You draw?' he asked in surprise.

Unable to answer for the loud hammering of her heart, she nodded.

He reached forward and plucked the pad from her nerveless fingers. Slowly, he thumbed through the pages. 'You're very talented,' he finally said.

Expecting a derogatory remark to follow, like his comment on his art this morning, her eyes widened when she realised he meant it. 'You really think so?' she asked.

He closed the pad and handed it back to her, his eyes speculative as they rested on her face. 'I wouldn't say it otherwise, *anjo*.'

Pleasure fizzed through her. 'Thank you.' She smiled as she stood. Crossing over to her duffel bag, she bent to place the pad back into it.

'*Thee mou!*'

She dropped the pad and hastily straightened. 'What?'

'You bend over like that while we're out and I will not be responsible for my actions, understood?' he growled.

Her mouth dropped open at the dark promise in his voice. A shudder ran through her body as hunger further darkened his eyes. She licked her lip nervously as the atmosphere thickened with sensual charges that crackled and snapped along her nerves.

'We…we don't have to go out if what I'm wearing offends you…Theo,' she ventured hesitantly, sensing that he held himself on the very edge of control.

He inhaled deeply, his chest expanding underneath the dark green shirt and black leather jacket he wore with black trousers. 'That's where you're wrong. What you're offering doesn't offend me in the least. But I'm a red-blooded, possessive male who is finding it difficult not to roar out his primitive reaction to the idea of other men looking at you.' He said it so matter-of-factly she couldn't form a decent response. 'But I'll try to be a *gentleman*. Come.' He held out his arm.

With seriously indecent thoughts of Theo fighting to the death for her flitting through her mind, she crossed the room to his side.

He led them out and held the passenger door of his car open. The first few minutes of the ride to Ipanema was conducted in silence. Every now and then, he raked a hand through his hair and slid a glance at her naked thighs. Each time, he exhaled noisily.

A wild part of her wanted to flaunt herself for him, revel in his very physical reaction to her attire. Another part of her wanted to run and hide from the volatile emotions swirling through the enclosed space of the luxurious sports car.

By the time they drew up in the car park of the exclusive restaurant her pulse was jumping with anxiety. She forced the feeling down and followed him into the restaurant. Finding out they were dining in the even more exclusive upper floor led to all sorts of renewed anxiety as she preceded him up the steps.

The moment they were seated, he leaned forward. 'The moment we return home, I'm burning those shorts.'

She glared at him. 'No, you are not, *senhor!* They're my favourite pair.'

'Then frame them and mount them on a wall. But you most definitely will not be wearing them out again.'

That wild streak widened. 'I thought you would be man enough to handle a little…challenge. Are you saying you're not?'

His eyes narrowed. 'Don't bait a hungry lion, *querida*, unless you're prepared to be devoured,' he grated out.

'Did you tell your last girlfriend how she should dress too?' she challenged.

His mouth compressed. 'My last girlfriend was under the misconception that the more frequently she walked around naked the more interested I would be in her. She lasted ten days.'

Inez's curiosity spiked, along with an emotion she was very loath to name. 'How long did your longest relationship last?'

'Three weeks.'

Her breath caught. 'So why three *months* with me?' she asked.

He looked startled for a moment then he shrugged. 'Because you're not my girlfriend. You're so very much more.'

Inez was struck dumb by his reply. A small foolish part of her even felt giddy, until she reminded herself that she was intended to be nothing but his *mistress*. Again unfathomable emotions wrapped themselves around her heart. She cleared her throat and fought to keep her voice even. 'Why *misconception*?'

'Very few women manage to catch and keep my interest for very long, *anjo*.'

'Because you get bored easily?' she dared.

His lashes swept down for a few seconds before they rose again to capture hers. 'Because my demons always win when pitted against the rigours of normal relationships.'

'*Demons*?'

'*Sim, anjo*. Demons. I have a lot of them. And they're very possessive.' A wave of anguish rolled over his face, then it was gone the next instant. He nodded to the hovering *sommelier* and ordered their wine. Another pulse of surprise went through her when she noticed it was the same wine she'd served at the fund-raiser and her favourite.

'The burning is now off the table. Hell, you can even keep the damn shorts. But, for the sake of my sanity, can we agree that you don't wear them outside?' he asked with one quirked eyebrow.

She pretended to consider it. 'What is your sanity worth to me?'

'You think you're in a position to bargain with me, Inez?' he asked, his voice deceptively soft.

'I never pass up an opportunity to bargain.'

He regarded her silently for several minutes. Then he shrugged. 'As long as I achieve my goals in the end, I see no reason why the road to success shouldn't be littered with minor obstacles. Tell me what you desire.'

'Is that what I am, a minor obstacle?'

'Don't miss your opportunity with meaningless questions.'

The need for clarity finally forced her to speak. 'I wish to know exactly what you want of me.'

'Sorry, I cannot answer that.'

She frowned. 'Why not?'

'Because my needs are…fluid.' The peculiar smile accompanying his answer sent a tingle of alarm down her spine.

'So I am to live in uncertainty for the next three months?'

'The unknown can be challenging. It can also be exciting.'

'Is that why you came to Rio? To seek challenge and excitement?'

For several seconds he stared at her. Then he slowly shook his head. 'No, my reason for being in Rio is specific and a well-planned event.'

Inez shivered at the succinct response. 'I can't help but be frightened by your answer.'

Her candid admission seemed to surprise him. 'Why is that?'

'Because I have a feeling it has something to do with my family. Pietro has his flaws but he's never done anything without my father's express approval. Besides, you're much older than him, which makes it unlikely that he's the one you came here for. You're here because of my father, aren't you?'

It took an astonishing amount of control not to react to her simple but accurate summation of the single subject that had consumed him for over a decade.

Thinking back, he realised he'd given her several clues to enable her to reach this conclusion. Somehow, in the mere forty-eight hours that he'd known her, Inez had managed to slip under his guard and was threatening to uncover his true purpose for being in Rio.

He also realised that he'd given her much more leeway than he'd ever intended to when he'd formulated his plan. Inviting her to compromise? Inviting her to state her desires with the knowledge that he was seriously considering granting them?

After his hasty departure this morning he'd realised that he'd let those marks on her arms sway him into going easy on her. *Because he hadn't wanted her to think he was a monster like her father?*

The man who hadn't so much as asked after his daughter when Theo had attended his office to sign the agreement papers?

The man whose eyes had shone with greed and triumph even before the ink had dried on the documents?

No, he was nothing like Benedicto da Costa. He wasn't about to lose any already precious sleep wondering about that little statement.

What he had to be careful of was that his enemy's daughter didn't guess his intentions. He was so very close to having Benedicto right where he wanted him. He couldn't afford to be swayed by a heart-shaped face or the most sinfully sexy pair of shorts he'd ever seen in his life, no matter how acute the ache in his groin.

'Will you please tell me why you're after my father?' she implored softly. The concern on her face appeared genuine and he suddenly realised that, despite Benedicto's treatment of her, Inez cared for her father.

His nostrils flared as bitterness rocked through him. He'd once been in that same position, foolishly believing that the father he'd idolised and loved beyond reason cared just as deeply for him. That he wasn't the fraudster and philanderer the press were making him out to be.

Now, he wanted to rip the blindfold from her eyes, make her see the true monster in the man she called *Pai*. Make her see that her love was nothing but a manipulative tool that would be used against her eventually.

Except he had a strong feeling she already knew, and chose to overlook it. Which made his blood boil even more.

'Why, do you plan to sacrifice yourself to save him?' he taunted.

She gasped, dropping the sterling silver fork she'd been nervously toying with. 'So, it *is* my father!'

He cursed under his breath. 'If you so much as breathe a word in his direction about your suspicions, I'll make sure you regret it for the rest of your life.'

She paled. 'You really expect me to sit back and watch you destroy him?'

'I expect you to hold up your end of the bargain we struck. Live under my roof in exchange for me leaving the loophole in the contract alone. Are you prepared to do that or do I need to plot another plan of action?' he asked, not bothering to hide the threat in his voice.

She stared back at him apprehensively. Her chin rose and her brown eyes burned holes in him but she nodded. 'I'll stick to our agreement.'

When their wine was served, he watched her take a big gulp and curbed the desire to follow suit. He was driving and needed to restrict his drinking. Nevertheless, a sip of the Chilean red went a way to restoring a little order to his floundering thoughts.

Thee mou, he hadn't even fired the first salvo and things were getting out of hand. Why on earth had he shared the presence of his demons with her? And that comment about her being so much more than a girlfriend? He silently shook his head and sucked in a control-affirming breath.

Their dinner progressed in near silence. Theo reminded himself that his main reason for bringing her out hadn't been for conversation. When she refused dessert, he settled the bill quickly and rose to help her out of her seat.

Fire shot through his groin, hard and fierce, as he was once again confronted with the risqué shorts. While they'd been seated, he'd managed to tamp down the effect of those shorts on his raging libido.

Now, as she walked in front of him, he was treated to a mouth-watering sight of her deliciously rounded bottom and stunning legs. With each sway of her hips, he grew harder until he wondered if he had any blood left in his upper extremities that hadn't migrated south.

He was reconsidering his decision not to burn the shorts at the earliest opportunity when he caught a male diner staring in blatant appreciation at her legs.

His growl was low but unmistakable. The man hastily averted his gaze but Theo was still simmering in primitive emotions when they reached the car park.

He followed her to the passenger side but, instead of opening the door for her, he braced his hand on either side of her and leaned in close. With her front pressed against the door, her bottom was moulded into his groin in such a way that she couldn't fail to notice his state of arousal.

Her breathing quickened, but she stayed put. 'What are you doing?'

'Delivering the punishment I promised.'

'Sorry?'

'You called me *senhor* when we were in the restaurant.'

She tried to turn around but he pressed her more firmly against the car. 'I…don't remember.'

'Of course you do. You also thought I wouldn't act on my promise in full view of other diners, didn't you?'

'No, I wasn't—'

'Maybe you were right. Or maybe we both knew I'd want to do more than just kiss you.'

'You're wrong…'

'Am I?'

'Yes…'

'So you'd prefer I let this one slide?' He rocked his hips against her bottom and her breath hitched. 'You won't think me weak?'

Her shocked laugh heated the air around them. 'Only someone foolish would think you weak.'

'I'm not sure whether there's a compliment in there. Is there?'

Her head fell forward, exposing the seductive line of her neck. 'Am I to pander to your ego too, Theo?'

He laughed. 'How can you appear submissive and yet taunt me at the same time?'

She lifted her head and turned to stare at him. Whatever she saw in his face made her squirm harder. Provocatively. Her gaze dropped to his mouth and Theo could no more resist the temptation than he could breathe.

Fingers sliding beneath her knotted hair to hold her still, he caught her mouth in a fierce kiss. Every emotion he'd experienced since waking that morning was delivered in that kiss—passion, arousal, confusion, anxiety and anger. He pinned her against the car so she couldn't move, couldn't put those seductive hands on his body.

Although he missed her touch, a part of him was thankful because, had she had access, he would've lost even more of his mind than he suspected he was losing.

He registered the brief flashes behind his closed eyelids but didn't break the kiss. He suspected Inez had no idea what had just happened. And even if she had, she wouldn't have suspected the true reason behind the paparazzi shots because she was used to being the darling of the press.

Well, she was in for a rude awakening...

She started to open her mouth wider, to return his demanding kiss.

He slowly lifted his head. When she made a tiny sound of protest and tried to recapture his mouth, he forced himself to step away. He'd achieved one part of what he'd set out to do. The second part was a short drive away.

Curving his arm around her waist, he peeled her away from the door, opened it and deposited her inside, all the time trying not to stare down at her legs and imagine how they would feel wrapped around his waist.

He swallowed hard as he rounded the hood and slid behind the wheel.

'Time to head to the club before I give in to the urge to deliver more punishment.'

Her eyes dropped to his mouth and he barely suppressed a groan as she licked her lips.

'For your mercy, I will teach you how to samba like a true Brazilian,' she replied huskily.

Inez lay among the white sheets the next morning, trying hard not to relive the events of the night before but it was as futile as trying to stop a tidal wave.

They'd eventually emerged from the nightclub at two in the morning. She'd been flushed and sweaty from being plastered to Theo's superb body for three straight hours. But the wild racing of her heart had nothing to do with her exertions on the dance floor and everything to do with the man who'd focused on her as if she was the only woman in the whole club.

And *Deus*, had he danced like a dream? Far from tutoring him on the correct steps of her native dance, she'd found herself following his lead as he'd moved expertly on the dance floor.

When he'd caught her to him, her back to his front and replayed the scene in the car park, but this time to music, she'd seriously feared her heart would beat itself to expiration.

In that moment, she'd forgotten that there was a sinister purpose to Theo's plan; that he'd all but admitted she was being used as a pawn in some deadly game he was playing with her father. When he'd laid his stubbled jaw against her cheek and hummed the sultry samba music in her ear, she'd closed her eyes and imagined what it would be like to belong—truly belong—to a man like Theo.

Turning over in bed, she groaned in disbelief at how

susceptible she'd been to his hard body and magnetic charisma. *Santa Maria*, she'd been all but putty in his hands.

Luckily, the fresh air and the long drive back had hammered some sense into her. The moment they'd returned, she'd bidden him a curt *boa noite*, left him standing in the hallway and retreated as fast as her sore feet would carry her.

And she intended to carry on like that. She might not know what his end game was, but she refused to be a willing participant in his campaign.

The last thing she wanted to do was to fall for another manipulator like Constantine.

She was here only because she had no choice but she didn't intend to idle away her time in this house. Theo expected her to stay here for three months, which meant whatever he had planned was not to be executed immediately. Perhaps she could convince him to change his mind in that time.

Yeah, and fairy tales really did come true…

Or she could find out exactly what his intentions were.

She'd seen the look in his eyes when he spoke about her father. Whatever vendetta he'd planned, he intended to see it through.

Helplessly, she rolled over in bed and her eyes lit on the bedside clock. She jerked upright and threw the sheet aside. She might not have anywhere to be on this Saturday morning but lazing about in bed past ten o'clock wasn't her style.

She jumped into the shower, shampooed her hair and washed her body with quick, regimented movement ingrained in her from her time at the Swiss boarding school her father had sent her to just to impress his friends.

Leaving her damp hair to dry naturally, she pulled on an aqua-coloured sundress and slipped her feet into low-heeled thongs. Smoothing her favourite sunscreen moisturiser over her face and arms, she left her room and headed downstairs.

Teresa was crossing the hallway carrying a *cafetière* of freshly made coffee and indicated for Inez to follow her.

She led her out to the terrace that overlooked the immense square infinity pool. Light danced off the water but her attention was caught and held by the man seated at the cast iron oval breakfast table.

His white short-sleeved polo shirt did amazing things to his eyes and olive-toned skin. And loose green shorts exposed solid thighs and lightly hair-sprinkled legs that made her mouth dry before flooding with moisture that threatened to choke her.

'*Bom dia, anjo*. Are you going to stand there all morning?' he mocked.

She forced her legs to move and took the chair he indicated to his right.

'Coffee?' he asked, his voice deep and low.

'Yes, please.' Her voice had grown husky and emerged barely above a whisper.

He nodded to Teresa who smiled, filled her cup then made herself scarce.

Inez sipped the hot brew just as a delaying tactic so she didn't have to look at him.

So far she'd seen Theo in formal evening wear and smart casual and each look had threatened to knock her sideways. But seeing him now, with so much of his vibrant olive skin on show, threatened to topple her completely. She took another hasty sip and choked as the liquid scalded her mouth.

Grabbing the napkin to stop herself from dribbling like an idiot, she looked up and caught his mocking smile. 'You'd rather blister yourself than converse with me?'

She swallowed and fought to present a passable smile. 'Of course not. I was just enjoying the…view.' She indicated beyond his shoulder, where the garden extended beyond the pool and sloped down to the sandy white beach and sparkling ocean.

With a disbelieving smile, he picked up the paper next to his plate and shook it out. 'If you say so—'

Her horrified gasp made him lower the newspaper. 'Something wrong?'

'Is that a picture of *us*?' she demanded through a severely constricted throat. The question was redundant because the picture taking up the whole of the front page was printed in vivid Technicolor.

He'd already seen it, of course, so he didn't bother to glance where her appalled gaze was riveted. 'Yes. Fresh off the morning press.'

'*Meu deus!*' She reached out and snatched the broadsheet out of his grasp. It was even worse up close. 'It looks as if...as if—' Disbelief caught in her throat, eating the rest of her words.

'As if I'm taking you from behind?' he supplied helpfully.

Humiliating heat stained her cheeks. '*Sim*,' she muttered fiercely. 'With your jacket covering me that way it looks as if I'm wearing nothing from the waist down! It's...it's disgusting!'

He plucked the paper from her hand and studied the picture. 'Hmm, it certainly is...*something*.'

'How can you sit there and be so unconcerned about it?' The picture had been taken with a high-resolution camera but, with the low lighting in the car park, the suggestiveness in the picture could be misinterpreted a thousand ways. None of them complimentary.

'Relax. We weren't exactly having sex, were we?'

'That's not the point.' She grabbed the paper back and quickly perused the article accompanying the gratuitous picture, fearing the worst. Sure enough, her father's political campaign had been called into question, along with an even more unsavoury speculation on her private life.

If this is what they do in public we can only imagine what they do in private...

Her hands shook as she threw the offending paper down.
'I thought this was a reputable paper.'

'It is.'

'Then why would they print something so...offensive?'

'Perhaps because it's true. We were kissing in the car
park. And you were pushing your delectable backside into
my groin as if you couldn't wait till we got home to do me.'

She surged to her feet, knocking her chair aside. Her
whole body was shaking with fury and she could barely
grasp the chair to straighten it.

'We both know I was not!'

'Do we? I told you those shorts were a bad idea. Do you
blame me for getting carried away?'

'Oh, you're *despicable!*'

'And you're delicious when you're angry,' he replied lazily, picked up the paper and carried on reading.

The urge to drive her fist through the paper into his face
made her take another hasty step back.

She abhorred violence. Or at least she had before she'd
met Theo Pantelides. Now she wasn't so sure what she was
capable of...

'Aren't you going to eat, *anjo*?' he asked without taking
his eyes off the page.

'No. I've lost my appetite,' she snapped.

She fled the terrace to the sound of his mocking laughter and raced up to her room, her face flaming and angry
humiliation smashing through her chest.

He found her on the beach an hour later. She heard the
crunch of his feet in the warm sand and studiously avoided
looking up. She carried on sketching the stationary boat an-
chored about a mile away and ignored him when he settled
himself on the flat rock next to her.

He didn't speak for a few minutes before he let out an
irritated breath. 'The silent treatment doesn't work for me,
Inez.'

She snapped her pad shut and turned to face him. His

lips were pinched with displeasure but his eyes were focused, gauging her reaction...almost as if her reaction mattered.

'Having my sex life sleazily speculated about in the weekend newspaper doesn't work for me either.' She blinked to dilute the intense focus and continued. 'I agree that perhaps those shorts were not the best idea. But I saw the other diners in that restaurant. There were people far more famous than I am. But still the paparazzo followed us into the car park and took our picture.'

Inez thought he tensed but perhaps it was the movement of his body as he reached behind him and produced a plate laden with food. 'It's done. Let's move on.'

She yearned to remain on her high horse, but with her exertions last night, coupled with having eaten less than a whole meal in the last twenty-four hours, it wasn't surprising when her stomach growled loudly in anticipation.

He shook out a napkin and settled the plate in her lap. 'Eat up,' he instructed and picked up her sketchpad. 'You have an hour before the stylist arrives to address the issue of your wardrobe.'

She froze in the act of reaching for the food. 'I don't need a stylist. I can easily go back home and pack up some more clothes.'

'You'll not be returning to your father's house for the next three months. Besides, if your clothes are all in the style of heavy evening gowns or tiny shorts, then you'll agree the time has come to go a different route?'

She mentally scanned her wardrobe and swiftly concluded that he was probably right. 'There really is no need,' she tried anyway.

'It's too late to change the plan, Inez.'

And, just like that, the subject was closed. He tapped the plate and, as if on cue, her stomach growled again.

Giving up the argument, she devoured the thick sliced beef sandwich and polished off the apple in greedy bites.

She was gulping down the bottled water when she saw him pause at her sketch of a boat.

'This is very good.'

'Thank you.'

He tilted the page. 'You like boats?'

'Very much. My mother used to take me sailing. It was my favourite thing to do with her.'

He closed the pad. 'Were you two close?'

'She was my best friend,' she responded in a voice that cracked with pain. 'Not a day goes by that I don't miss her.'

His fingers seemed to tighten on the rock before they relaxed again. 'Mothers have a way of affecting you that way. It makes their absence all the harder to bear.'

'Is yours…when did you lose yours?' she asked.

He turned and stared at her. A bleak look entered his eyes but dissolved in the next blink. 'My mother is very much alive.'

She gasped. 'But I thought you said…'

'Absence doesn't mean death. There are several ways for a parent to be absent from a child's life without the ultimate separation.'

'Are you talking about abandonment?'

Again he glanced at her, and this time she caught a clearer glimpse of his emotions. Pain. Devastating pain.

'Abandonment. Indifference. Selfishness. Self-absorption. There are many forms of delivering the same blow,' he elaborated in a rough voice.

'I know. But I was lucky. My mother was the best mother in the world.'

'Is that why you're trying to be the best daughter in the world for your father, despite what you know of him?'

His accusation was like sandpaper against her skin. 'I beg your pardon?'

He shook his head. 'Don't bother denying it. You know exactly what sort of person he is. And yet you've stood by him all these years. Why—because you want a pat on the head and to be told you're a good daughter?'

The truth of his words hit her square in the chest. Up until yesterday, everything she'd done, every plan of her father's she'd gone along with had been to win his approval, and in some way make up for the fact that she hadn't been born the right gender. She didn't want to curl up and hide from the truth. But the callous way he condemned her made her want to justify her actions.

'I'm not blind to my father's shortcomings.' She ignored his caustic snort. 'But neither am I going to make excuses for my actions. My loyalty to my family isn't something I'm ashamed of.'

'Even when that loyalty meant turning a blind eye to other people's suffering?' he demanded icily.

She frowned. 'Whose suffering?'

'The people he left behind in the *favelas* for a start. Do you know that less than two per cent of the funds raised at those so-called charity events you so painstakingly put together actually make it to the people who need it most?'

She felt her face redden. His condemning gaze raked over her features. 'Of course you do,' he murmured acidly.

'It happened in the past, I admit it, but I only agreed to organise the last event if everything over and above the cost of doing it went to the *favelas*.' At his disbelieving look, she added, 'I do a lot of work with charities. I know what I'm talking about.'

'And did you ensure that it was done?'

'Yes. The charity confirmed they'd received the funds yesterday.'

One eyebrow quirked in surprise before he jerked to his feet. Thrusting his hands into his pockets, he turned to face her. 'That's progress at least.'

'Thank you. I don't live in a fairy tale. Trust me, I'm trying to do my part to help the *favelas*.'

'How?'

She debated a few seconds before she answered. 'I work at an inner city charity a few times a week.'

His gaze probed hers. 'That morning outside the coffee shop, that was where you were going?'

'Yes.'

'What does your father think?'

She bit her lip. 'He doesn't know.'

His mouth twisted. 'Because it will draw attention to his lies about his upbringing? Everyone knows he was born and raised in the *favelas*.'

'It's part of the reason why I didn't tell him, yes. But he denies his *favela* upbringing because he's…ashamed.'

'And yet he doesn't mind anyone knowing about his mother?'

'He thinks it gives him a little leverage with the common man to be indirectly associated with the *favelas*.'

'So he likes to rewrite his history as he goes along?'

'Perhaps. I don't delude myself for one second that my father doesn't bend the rules and the truth at times.'

His harsh laugh made her start. 'Right. Are you talking about, oh, let's see…doing ninety on a sixty miles per hour road, or are we talking about something with a little more…teeth?'

That note she'd heard before. The one that sent a foreboding chill along her spine, that warned her that something else was going on here. Something she should be running far and fast from. 'I…I'm not sure what you're implying.'

'Then let me spell it out for you. Are we talking about harmless anecdotes or are we talking about actual deeds? You know—broken kneecaps? Ruptured spleens. *Kidnap for ransom*?'

Her hand flew to her mouth. 'What the hell are you talking about?'

'Come on, you know what your father is capable of. Do

I need to remind you of what he did to you when you displeased him?'

She followed his gaze to the marks on her arm and slowly shook her head. 'I don't excuse this but I refuse to believe he's the monster you describe.'

His mouth twisted. 'I'll let you enjoy your rosy outlook for now, *querida*. I, too, felt like that once about my own father.'

'Is that what you're going to do to my father? Make him accountable for the things he's done?'

For several heartbeats she was sure he wouldn't answer her, or would change the subject the way he'd done in the past. But finally he nodded.

'Yes. I intend to make him pay for what he took from me twelve years ago.'

Her breath froze in her lungs. 'What did he take from you?'

He turned abruptly and faced the water, his stance rigid and forbidding. But Inez found herself moving towards him anyway, a visceral need driving her. She reached out and touched his shoulder. He tensed harder and she was reminded of his reaction to her touch on his boat. 'Theo?'

'I don't like being touched when my back's turned, *anjo*.'

She frowned. 'Why not?'

'Part of my demons.'

Her gut clenched hard at the rough note in his voice. 'Did…did my father do that to you?'

'Not personally. After all, he's an upright citizen now, isn't he? A man the people should trust.' He whipped about to face her.

'But he had something to do with your claustrophobia. And this?'

'Yes.'

'Theo—'

'Enough with the questions! You're forgetting why you're here. Do you need a reminder?'

She swallowed at the arctic look in his eyes. All signs of the raw, vulnerable pain she'd glimpsed minutes ago were wiped clean. Theo Pantelides was once again a man in control, bent on revenge. Slowly, she shook her head. 'No. No, I don't.'

CHAPTER EIGHT

THEIR CONVERSATION AT the beach set a frigid benchmark for the beginning of her stay at Theo's glass mansion.

The next two weeks passed in an icy blur of hectic days and even more hectic evenings. They'd quickly fallen into a routine where Theo left after a quick cup of coffee and a brief outline of when and where they would be dining that evening.

On the second morning when she'd told him she was heading for the charity, he'd raised an eyebrow. 'What sort of work do you do there?'

'Whatever I'm needed to do.' She'd been reluctant to tell him any specifics in case he disparaged her efforts as a rich girl's means of passing the time till the next party.

He'd returned to his coffee. 'Your time is your own when I'm not around. As long you're back here when I return, I see no problem.'

That had been the end of the subject.

After repeating his warning not to mention anything to her father he'd walked away. The man who'd shown her his pain and devastation had completely retreated.

His demeanour during their time indoors was icily courteous. However, when they went out, which they did most evenings, he was the attentive host, touching her, threading his fingers through her hair and gazing adoringly at her.

It was after the fifth night out that she realised he was

pandering to the paparazzi. Without fail, a picture of them in a compromising position appeared in the newspapers the very next morning.

But while she cringed with every exposing photo, he shrugged it off. It wasn't until her third weekend with him, when the newspapers posted the first poll results of the mayoral race, that she finally had her suspicions confirmed.

He was swimming in the pool, his lean and stunning body cutting through the water like the sleekest shark. The byline explaining the reasons behind the voters' reaction had her surging to her feet and storming to the edge of the pool.

'Is this why you've been taking me out every night since I moved in? So I'd be labelled the slut daughter of a man not fit to be mayor?' She raised her voice loud enough to be heard above his powerful strokes.

He stopped mid-stroke, straightened and slicked back his wet hair. With smooth breaststrokes he swam to where she stood barefoot. Looking down at his wet, sun-kissed face, she momentarily lost her train of thought.

He soon set her straight. 'Your father isn't worthy to lead a chain gang, never mind a city,' he replied in succinct, condemning tones. 'And before I'm done with him, the whole world will know it.'

Despite seeing the evidence for herself two weeks ago at the beach, despite knowing that whatever her father had done to him had been devastating, she staggered back a step at that solid, implacable oath.

He planted his hands on the tiles and heaved himself out of the water. It took every ounce of her self-control not to devour him with hungry eyes. But not looking didn't mean not feeling. Her insides clenched with the ever-growing hunger she'd been unable to stem since the first night he'd walked into her life. And, with each passing day, she was finding it harder and harder to remain unaffected.

It seemed not even knowing why she was here, or the full extent of how Theo intended to use her to hurt her fa-

ther, could cause her intense emotional reaction to his prox-
imity to abate.

Which made her ten kinds of a fool, who needed to pull
her thoughts together or risk getting hurt all over again.

'So you don't deny that you used me as bait to derail my
father's campaign?'

Hazel eyes, devoid of emotion, narrowed on her face.
'That was one course of action. But you haven't been labelled a slut. I'll sue any newspaper that dares to call you
that,' he rasped.

Her laughter scraped her throat. 'There are several ways
to describe someone without using the actual derogatory
word, Theo.'

He paused in drying his hair and looked at her. Slowly,
he held out his hand. 'Show me.'

She handed the paper over. He read it tight-jawed. 'I'll
have them print a retraction.'

Dismay roiled through her stomach, along with a heavy
dose of rebellious anger.

'That's not the point, though, is it? The harm's already
done. You know this means I'll have to stop volunteering,
don't you? I can't bring this sort of attention to the charity.'

He frowned and she caught a look of unease on his face.
'I'll take care of this.'

'Forget it; it's too late. And congratulations; you've
achieved your aim. But I won't be paraded about and pawed
in public any more, so if you're planning on another night
on the town you'll have to do it without me.'

His gaze slowly rose to hers and he resumed rubbing the
towel through his hair. 'Fine. We'll do something else.' He
threw the paper on the table.

She regarded him suspiciously. 'Something like what?'

'I promised you a trip on the yacht. We'll sail this evening and spend tomorrow aboard. Would you like that?'

At times like these, when he was being a courteous host,

she found it hard to believe he was the same man who was hell-bent on seeking revenge on her father for past wrongs.

She'd given in to her gnawing curiosity after his revelations on the beach and searched the Internet for a clue as to what had happened to him. All she'd come up with were scant snippets of his late father's dirty dealings before Alexandrou Pantelides had died in prison. As far as she knew, there was no connection between Theo's family and hers. The Pantelides brothers, one of whom was married and recently a parent, and the other engaged to be married, were a huge success in the oil, shipping and luxury hotel world. Theo's job as a troubleshooter extraordinaire for the billion-dollar conglomerate meant he never settled in one place for very long. An ideal job for a man whose personal relationships were fleeting at best.

And a man tormented by a horde of demons.

She looked closer at him, tried to see the man behind the wall, the man who'd bared his soul for a brief moment when he'd spoken of his mother's abandonment.

But that man was closed off.

'What does it matter what I want? Frankly, I'm surprised my father hasn't been in touch about this.'

'He has. I refused to take his calls.'

'I didn't mean you. Since I was also the subject in these photos, I'm surprised he hasn't called me to vent his anger.'

His eyelids swept down and shielded his gaze from her. Apprehension struck a jagged path through her. 'He has, hasn't he?'

'He tried. I suggested that perhaps he refrain from contacting you and concentrate on kissing babies and convincing little old ladies to cast their ballot in his favour.'

Shock rooted her to the ground. 'How dare you take control of my life like this?'

'Would you rather I gave him access so he airs his disappointment?'

'What do you care? It's a little late to protect me, don't you think?'

His jaw tightened. 'For as long as you remain under my roof, you're under my protection.'

'*Meu deus*, please don't pretend you care!'

She realised how close she was to tears and swallowed hard. Fearing she would break down in front of him, she whirled round, intent on heading for her room. She made it two steps before he stopped her.

Flinging away the towel, he cupped her cheeks with both hands. 'Stop getting yourself distressed about this.'

'Is that another command?'

His eyes narrowed. 'You're angry.'

'Damn right I am. I wish I'd never set eyes on you. In fact I wish—'

His mouth slanted over hers, hot, hungry and all consuming. Her groan of protest was less than heartfelt and devoured within a millisecond.

A part of her was furious that he'd resorted to kissing her to shut her up. But it was only a minuscule part. The rest of her body was too busy revelling in the feel of his warm bare back and the fine definition of muscles that rippled beneath her caress.

His hands speared into her hair, imprisoning her for the invasion of his tongue as he took the kiss to another level.

His first kiss over two weeks ago had been a pure threat and the two that followed a show of mastery. This kiss was different. There was hunger and passion behind it, but also a gentleness that calmed her roiling emotions and slowly replaced them with a different sensation. Need clamoured inside her; a need to be closer still to his magnificent body; a need to dig her hands into his back and feel him shudder in reaction.

His groan was smothered between their melded lips as she dug her fingers even deeper. Power surged through her when he jerked again.

One hand dropped to her bottom and yanked her lower body into his groin. His erection was unmistakable. Bold, thick and hot, it pressed against her belly with insistent power that made her heartbeat skitter out of control.

She wanted him. Above and beyond all sense, she wanted this man. Her willpower, when it came to the chemistry between them, was laughably negligible.

But she couldn't give in. *Couldn't…*

The gentleness she'd sensed in him was false, she reminded herself fiercely. The bottom line was that in a few short weeks he would walk away. Leave her and her family devastated.

'I'm losing you. Come back, *anjo*,' he murmured seductively against her mouth. He ran his tongue over her lower lip and her knees weakened.

When he cupped her bottom and squeezed, she desperately summoned all her resolve and pushed against his chest. 'No.'

He raised his head and she saw behind the wall. He was as caught in this insane chemistry as she was. A little part of her felt better.

'I can change your mind, Inez. Regardless of what I intend for your father, what is between us is undeniable.'

'Do you hear yourself? You think I should forget everything else and sleep with you just because you made me feel a certain way?'

'That's generally the reason why men and women have sex.'

'But we're not just any man and any woman, Theo, are we?'

He stiffened, and a hard look entered his eyes. 'Are you saying that you've been in love with every man you've slept with?' he queried.

She froze and prayed her humiliation wouldn't show on her face as she tried to stem the memory of Constantine's treatment of her.

His cruel rejection was still an ache beneath her breastbone.

'Inez?' Theo interjected harshly.

'My past relationships are none of your business.'

His slightly reddened mouth twisted. 'Far be it for me to request to be lumped in with your other lovers, but isn't it a touch hypocritical to apply one criteria to me that you haven't done with one of your lovers, in particular?'

'If you're referring to Constantine, let me assure you that you have no idea what you're talking about.'

His hand tightened around her waist. 'Then enlighten me. Why did he dump you?'

Inez broke free. 'We weren't compatible.'

'Or he found out the true reason you were with him and wanted nothing to do with you?'

'No. That wasn't why…' She screeched to a stop as the words stuck in her throat.

'So what was it? Did you really love him or did you convince yourself you did in order to achieve your aims?'

She bit her lip as he shone a light on the stark question. Had she blown her feelings out of proportion? Constantine had been charismatic, yes, but he'd never created the decadent chaos that Theo created in her.

When she'd imagined love, she'd always imagined passion, hunger and a keen pleasure even the slightest thought of that special someone brought. She'd believed herself in love with Constantine and yet she'd never experienced those emotions.

Well, she most definitely wasn't feeling them now.

'I believed my emotions were genuine at the time. But he didn't. He believed I was using him to further my father's campaign.'

'What did he do?' he asked. She looked into his eyes and fooled herself into thinking she saw a thawing of the hardness there.

'He made painful digs at me whenever he gave interviews. He made the tabloids call my character into question…much the same way you're doing now.'

He dropped his hand. 'It's not the same—'

'Yes, it is. Look Theo, I just want to be left alone to do my time.'

He paled. 'You're not in prison, Inez.'

She put much needed distance between them. 'Am I not? How else would you describe my presence here?'

Theo watched her walk away and curled his fists at his sides. The urge to call her back was so strong he forced himself to exhale slowly to expel the need. Her reference to her presence under his roof as a prison sentence had stung badly.

But hell, the truth was irrefutable. He'd forced her to make a choice, and no amount of dinner dates or designer shopping sprees would gloss over the fact that he'd set the tabloids on her as a way to dismantle her father's campaign.

Witnessing her clear distress just now had made his chest ache in a way that confused and irritated him.

Perhaps he needed to step up his agenda, end this dangerous game once and for all and move on with his life.

His brothers would certainly agree. He'd been avoiding their calls for the best part of a fortnight, replying only by email and with curt one-liners that he knew would only go so far before something gave.

He gritted his teeth against the prompt to deliver a swift killing blow to Benedicto da Costa.

His own ordeal hadn't been swift. It'd been long and tortuous. The punishment should fit the crime. Any hesitation on his part now merely stemmed from the afterglow of the chemistry between him and Inez. He freely admitted that theirs was a strong and potent brand, more intense than anything he'd ever experienced before.

It was messing with his mind, the same way the thought of her ex-lover had made him see red for several long seconds. But there was no way he was letting it impede his goal.

Which meant he had to come at this problem from another angle.

He swallowed the acrid taste in his mouth at the thought that Inez had put him into the same class as Constantine Blanco.

Slowly walking back indoors, he turned over the dilemma in his mind. By the time he reached his suite and changed out of his swimming trunks, a smile was curving his lips.

An hour later, he watched her descend the stairs, her duffel bag slung over her shoulder and an overnight case in her hand.

'Did Teresa tell you to pack your swimming gear?'

She regarded him warily. 'Yes. But I thought we were just taking the boat out?'

He shrugged. 'I thought you would welcome the opportunity to sunbathe away from the prying lenses of the paparazzi? There are several decks on the yacht that you can sunbathe on. Or we can swim in the sea, dine alone under the stars. Would you like that?' he asked, then felt a jolt at how much he wanted her to answer in the affirmative. In the past, he'd never taken the time to seek out what pleased his girlfriends beyond the usual gifts and fine dining. It was why he operated his relationships on a strict short-term basis with as little maintenance as possible.

Inez was far from low maintenance. And yet he found himself even more drawn to her.

She glanced pointedly over his shoulder. 'I'll think about it and let you know.'

His unsettled feelings escalated. He reminded himself that they were heading for his boat. She liked his boat. Perhaps she would relent enough to forget that she was angry with him. Forget about Blanco and forget that she was being blackmailed.

Theo was still debating why her feelings meant so much to him when he pulled up at the marina.

* * *

'You've been smiling ever since we set sail.'

Her voice was full of heavy suspicion. Theo's smile widened as he tilted his face up into the sunshine. 'Have I? It must be the weather.'

'The weather has been the same for the last month,' she replied sourly.

He slowly lowered his head and captured her gaze with his. 'Then it must be the company.'

A delicate wave of heat surged up her neck into her cheeks, making him wonder, as he had more than once these past two weeks, how she could have been involved with someone like Blanco and still blush like a schoolgirl.

Theo had looked into Constantine Blanco and had not been surprised to find that he was cut from the same cloth as Benedicto. It was perhaps why Da Costa had chosen to ally himself with the younger man politically. He'd sent his daughter to spy on Blanco and had been double-crossed in the bargain.

Theo's smile slipped as he recalled her hurt when he'd thrown her relationship with Blanco at her. He reached for the glass of wine that had accompanied their late afternoon meal and took a large gulp.

The guilt tightening in his chest since her accusation at the pool squeezed harder.

What the hell was going on with him?

'Have you decided whether you're selling the boat or not?' she asked.

In the sunlight, her black hair gleamed like polished jet, making him burn to feel its silkiness beneath his fingers.

He stared into his drink. 'Maybe. I'll have to weigh up practical usage versus the desire to hang on to something beautiful.'

'But you're a billionaire. Isn't collecting toys part and parcel of your status?'

'I wasn't always a man of means. In fact my brothers and

I worked our backsides off to achieve the level of success we enjoy now.' His smile felt tight and strained.

'Your brothers…Sakis and Arion…'

He looked up in surprise. 'You've been playing around on the Internet, I see.'

She raised her chin. 'I thought it wise to learn a little bit more about my enemy.'

The label grated. Badly. 'What else did you try to discover while you were rooting around my family tree?'

'Your brother Sakis had some trouble with a saboteur on one of his oil tankers.'

He nodded. 'We dealt with that quite satisfactorily.'

'And now your brother Ari is engaged to the widow of the man who tried to throw your company into chaos?' She frowned.

A reluctant grin tugged at his mouth. 'What can I say; we thrive on interesting challenges.'

'You also seem to make enemies with the people you do business with. So far you've led me to believe it was my father who wronged you. How do I know it's not the other way round? That you're not here because you deserved everything you got?'

The stem of the wine glass snapped with a sickening crack. Even then it took the cold wine seeping into his shirt to realise what he'd done.

The top part of the glass landed on the table, rolled off and smashed onto the deck.

Inez gasped. 'Theo, you're bleeding!' She surged to her feet and sprang towards him.

'Stop!'

'But your finger…'

'Is nothing compared to what will happen to your foot if you take another step.'

She glanced down at the broken glass an inch from her bare foot and glanced back at his bleeding forefinger. Anguish creased her pale features.

'Sit down, Inez,' he instructed tersely.

'Please, let me help,' she implored.

Gritting his teeth, he grabbed a napkin and formed a small tourniquet around the gaping wound. 'It's not deep but will need to be cleaned properly. There's a first aid kit behind the bar.'

She nodded, slipped on her sandals and dashed for the bar. Theo stood and moved from the dining table to the wraparound sofa to give the crew member who'd arrived on deck room to sweep up the broken glass. He glanced up as Inez rushed back and set the kit on the coffee table.

Her eyes were turbulent with worry as she glanced from his face to the blood-soaked napkin.

'Are you going to stand there staring at me all evening? I'm bleeding to death here.'

With a hoarse croak, she jerked into action. She carefully cleaned the wound with antiseptic and applied gauze before securing it with a plaster. All through the procedure, she darted quick, apologetic glances at him.

As he stared at her, he felt a different sort of jolt run through him. One he hadn't been aware he was missing until he felt it.

Care. Concern. Fear for him.

When was the last time anyone besides Ari and Sakis had felt like that about him? When was the last time his own mother lavished such attention on him? Inez slid him another worried glance and his breath shuddered out.

'Calm yourself, *anjo*. I'll live. I'm sure of it.'

She exhaled noisily and her agitated pulse pounded at her throat. '*Sinto muito*,' she said in a rush.

'Don't apologise. It wasn't your fault.'

'But…if I hadn't accused you of…'

'You're operating in the dark and want to find out the truth. I respect that. But I can't tell you what my business with your father is until I'm ready. You have to respect that.'

'But…this…' She glanced down at his finger and shook

her head. 'Your reaction…the claustrophobia and the touching thing…I can't help but fear the worst, Theo,' she whispered.

Against his will, his chest constricted at the anguish in her voice. He wanted to comfort her. Wanted to take that look of anticipated pain from her face. He wanted to kiss her until they both forgot why she was his prisoner and why he was beginning to dread the day he had to set her free.

He swallowed hard.

'Let's make a deal. For the next twenty-four hours, no talk of your father or the reason why I'm in Rio. Agreed?'

Her mouth wobbled and her teeth worried her bottom lip as she glanced back at his finger. Her eyes were no less turbulent when they rose to his but he saw determination flare in their depths. 'Agreed.'

Theo stood at the railing on the third floor deck and watched her swim in the pool on the second deck the next morning. She moved like a water nymph, her long black hair streaming down her back as she scissored her arms and legs underwater.

He gripped the rail until his knuckles turned white but still he couldn't take his eyes off her.

'I'm waiting for an answer, Theo,' came the weary voice at the end of the line.

Theo sighed. 'Sorry, remind me again what the question was.'

Ari grunted with annoyance. 'I asked you why I couldn't have one peaceful breakfast without opening the papers to find you wrapped around some poor girl. Seriously, my digestive system has sent me a stern memo. Either I treat it better and not subject it to such images or it goes on permanent vacation.'

Theo heard Perla, his soon-to-be sister-in-law, laughing in the background.

'The answer is simple. Don't read the papers.'

Ari sighed. 'How long is this going to go on for?'

'Everything should be signed, sealed and delivered in a week or two,' he responded, rolling his shoulders to ease the tension tightening his muscles. Another sleepless night, plagued with nightmares. He'd given up on sleep somewhere around three a.m.

'You sound very sure.'

His grip tightened around the phone. As he'd lain awake he'd briefly toyed with the idea of ending this vendetta sooner. And he'd been stunned when the idea had taken firm hold. 'I am.'

'And nothing you're doing down there will affect the wedding? Don't forget it's in two weeks. If you can prise yourself away from that piece of skirt for long enough—'

'She's not a piece of skirt,' he snarled before he could catch his response. Ari's silence made him hurry to speak. 'I'll be at your wedding.'

'Good, since you've missed most of the rehearsals, I'll send you the video of what you need to do. Make sure you get it right; we'll do a quick rehearsal when you get here. I'm not having you mess things up for Perla.'

'Sure. Fine,' he murmured.

He followed the curvy, sexy shape underneath the water and held his breath as Inez broke the surface and rose out of the pool. Dripping curves and sun-kissed skin made his body clench unbearably. He wanted to trace every single inch of her with his hands, his mouth, his tongue. 'Oh, and tell Perla I'm bringing a guest.'

His brother muttered a curse and relayed the message. Theo heard Perla's whoop of delight. 'The love of my life grudgingly agrees but suggests that perhaps, next time, you could be courteous enough to give us a heads-up sooner?'

'Next time? You mean you'll be getting married for a third time?'

He hung up to more pithy curses ringing in his ears and found himself smiling. Without taking his eyes off the figure below, he descended the spiral staircase and walked towards the bikini-clad goddess reaching for the towel on the shelf next to the pool.

Her back was turned and he slowed to a stop as the sight of her tiny waist and curvy hips made blood rush through his veins. Lust twisted through his gut, hard and demanding.

Hell, this was getting unbearable.

He threw his cell phone on the breakfast table and watched her jerk around to face him. The towel she was holding to her hair stilled.

'Hi.'

'Good morning. Enjoy your swim?'

'It was very refreshing,' she replied huskily, her eyes following him warily as he strode towards her. 'So, what's the plan for today?' she asked.

I want to haul you off to my bed and keep you underneath me until we both pass out from the pleasure overload.

He wrenched his gaze from her full breasts, lovingly cupped by damp white triangles, and concentrated on breathing. 'We're headed for Copacabana. We'll stop for something to eat then head back tonight. Or if you want we can stay on the boat and leave in the morning?'

She thought about it for a second and nodded. 'I'd love to draw the boat in the moonlight.'

'Then that's what you shall do.'

Her gaze turned puzzling, weighing.

'What's on your mind?' he asked.

She shook her head slightly and slowly folded the towel. 'Sometimes I feel as if I'm dealing with two people.'

Something hard tugged in his chest. 'Which one do you prefer?'

'Are you joking? The person you are now, of course.'

He froze as the tug tightened its hold on him. His breath came in short pants as he closed the distance between them. 'I thought we weren't going to delve into our issues today.'

'You asked me what was on my mind.'

He nodded. 'I guess I did.' He stared into the pure, make-up-free perfection of her face and something very close to regret rose in his gut.

'Now it's my turn to ask you what's on your mind, Theo,' she murmured thoughtfully.

'It's completely pointless, of course, but I'm wishing we'd met under different circumstances.'

Her mouth dropped open. 'You are?'

The urge to touch grew, and he finally gave in. He traced his thumb over her lips and felt them pucker slightly under his touch. 'As I said, it's pointless.'

'Because you would've been done with me within a week?' she ventured.

'No. I would've kept you for much longer, *anjo*. Perhaps even for ever.'

He forced himself to step away. Once again she'd slid so effortlessly under his skin, opened him up to wishes and possibilities he'd forced himself never to entertain after what their respective fathers and his mother had done to him. She was making him believe in impossible dreams, feelings he had no business experiencing.

He strode quickly towards the pool. A cold dip would wash away the fiery need and alien emotions tearing his insides to shreds. He hoped.

He emerged twenty minutes later to find her polishing off the last of her scrambled eggs and coffee. Over the past fortnight he'd noticed that she ate with a gusto that triggered his own appetite. Or *appetites*.

As he poured his coffee and helped himself to fruit, she reached for the ever-present duffel bag and pulled out her sketchpad.

'Have you thought of doing something with your talent?' he asked.

A shadow passed over her face before she tried to smile through it, but he guessed the reason behind it. Her father.

'I will once I resume my education. I put pursuing my degree on hiatus for a while.'

He didn't need to ask why. 'Until when?'

She shrugged and searched for a fresh page in her pad. 'I haven't decided yet.'

Theo tried not to let his anger show. They'd called a truce for twenty-four hours.

'What will you study when you return?'

'I love buildings and boats. I may go into architecture or boat design.'

He glanced from her face to the pad. 'Boat design, huh?' She nodded.

He picked up his coffee and regarded her over the rim. 'Why don't you design me one?'

'You want me to design a boat for you?'

'Yes. I'm sure your research showed you what sort of designs we specialise in. It has to be up to the Pantelides standard. But use your own template. Make it state-of-the-art, of course.'

'Of course,' she murmured but he could see the gleam of interest in her eyes as she stared down at her pad.

Her pencil flew across the paper as he devoured his breakfast. She didn't look up as he rose and rounded the table to where she sat. He didn't glance down at her drawing; he was too absorbed with the sheer joy on her face as she became immersed in her task.

Even when his finger drifted down her cheek to the corner of her mouth she barely glanced up at him. But her breath hitched and she jerked a tiny bit towards his touch before he withdrew his hand.

As he walked away, Theo marvelled at how light-hearted he felt.

CHAPTER NINE

THEY DROPPED ANCHOR about a mile away from Copacabana Beach and took a launch ashore.

Inez looked to where Theo stood, legs braced, at the wheel of the launch. The wind rushed through his dark hair, whipping it across his forehead. Stupid that she should be jealous of the wind but she clenched her fingers in her lap as they tingled with the need to touch him.

I would've kept you for much longer, anjo. *Perhaps even for ever.*

Try as she had for the last few hours, she couldn't get his words out of her head. They struck her straight to the heart in unguarded moments, made her breath catch in ways that made her dizzy. Every time she pushed the feeling away. But, inevitably, it returned.

She was in serious trouble here…

A shout from nearby sunbathers drew her attention to the fact that they were not alone any more.

She watched the surge of people and the noise of tourists enjoying a Sunday stroll along the beach roads and suddenly felt as if she was losing the tenuous connection she'd made with Theo last night and this morning. Which was silly. There was no connection. Just a precarious truce.

And an exciting task designing a Pantelides boat, which had made joy bubble beneath her skin all day.

He brought the launch to a smooth stop at the pier and

turned off the engine. Jumping out with lithe grace, he held out his hand to her, the smile on his face making her breath stutter in her chest as she slipped her hand into his.

'I'm in the mood for some traditional food and I know just the place for it. You happy to trust me?'

Safely on solid ground, she glanced up and found herself nodding. 'Yes.'

His eyes darkened. 'It's a bit of a walk.' He glanced at her high-heeled wedges with a cocked eyebrow.

'Don't worry about me. I was born in heels.'

'Then I pity your poor *mãe*.'

She laughed and saw his answering smile.

Gradually they fell silent and his gaze drifted over her face, resting on her mouth for a few seconds before he tugged on her hand. 'Come on, *anjo*.'

He led her along the pier and towards the streets. Ten minutes later, she stared in surprise when they stopped outside a door with a faded sign and a single light bulb above it.

'I hear they serve the best *feijoadas* in Rio,' he said, his gaze probing her every expression.

Inez forced the lump in her throat down as she stared at the sign that had been very much part of a long ago, happier childhood. 'It's true. I…how do you know about this place?'

The hand he'd captured since they alighted from the boat meshed with hers, causing her heart to flutter wildly as he brought it to his lips and kissed the back of it. 'I made it my business to find out.'

Again tears choked her and she couldn't speak for several moments. 'Thank you.'

He nodded. 'My pleasure.'

They stopped in the doorway to allow their eyes to adjust to the candlelit interior.

'*Pequena estrela!*' A matronly woman in her late forties approached, her face lit up with a smile.

After exchanging hugs, Inez turned to introduce Theo.

'Camila and my mother were best friends. I used to have supper here many times after school when I was a kid.'

Theo responded to the introduction in smooth, charming Portuguese that had the older woman blushing before she led them to a table in the middle of the room.

'You want the usual?' Camila asked after she'd brought over a basket of bread and taken their wine order.

Inez glanced at Theo. 'Will you let me choose?'

He sat back in his chair, his gaze brushing her face. 'It's your show, *anjo*.'

She rattled off the order and added a few more dishes that had Camila nodding in approval before she bustled off.

Alone with Theo, she tried to calm her giddy senses. Not read too much into why he'd brought her here of all places. But her emotions refused to be calmed.

He was making her feel things she had no business feeling, considering their circumstances. Her heart was very much in danger of being devastated. And this time the danger signs were not disguised as they'd been with Constantine. She was walking into this with her heart and eyes wide open…

'You're frowning too hard, *querida*.'

Plucking a piece of bread from the basket, she fought to focus on not ruining their truce. 'I think I may have ordered too much food.'

'You have a healthy appetite. Nothing wrong with that.'

'It's that healthy appetite that keeps me on the wrong side of chubby.'

'You're not chubby. You're perfect.'

Her hand stilled on the way to her mouth. In the ambient light, she witnessed the potent, knee-weakening look of appreciation on his face. The look slowly grew until hunger became deeply etched into his every feature.

Desire pounded through her, sending radial pulses of heat through her body to concentrate on that needy place between her legs. '*Obrigado*,' she murmured hoarsely.

He nodded slowly, leant forward and took the piece of bread from her hand. Tearing off a piece, he held it against her mouth. When she opened it, he placed it on her tongue and watched her chew.

Then he sat back and ate the remaining piece.

She eventually managed to swallow and cast around for a safe topic of conversation that didn't involve her father or the dangerous emotions arcing between them.

Whether he noticed her floundering or not, she smiled gratefully when he asked, 'Did your mother grow up around here?'

'No, both she and Camila grew up near the Serra Geral, although she spent part of her childhood in Arizona where my grandmother was from. Their fathers were ranch-owning *gauchos* and neighbours but after they both married they moved to Rio and stayed in touch. Camila is like a second mother to me...'

'Da Costa Holdings isn't a cattle business, though,' he replied, then stiffened slightly.

She smiled quickly, wanting to hold onto the animosity-free atmosphere they'd found. 'No, after my grandfather died, my mother sold the ranch and let my father expand the company instead.' She breathed in relief when Camila returned with their wine and first course.

The older woman's warm smile and effusive manner further lightened the mood. By the time she took her first sip of the bold red wine the slightly chilly interlude had passed.

Theo complimented her on the food choice and tucked into the grilled fish starter. The conversation returned to safer topics and eventually turned to his previous career as a championship-winning rower.

'Why did you stop competing?'

He shrugged. 'I tried a few partners after Ari and Sakis retired. The chemistry was lacking. In a sport like that chemistry is key.' He topped up her wine and took a sip of his own.

'You've been lucky to have had the opportunity to do something you loved,' she replied wistfully.

His smile looked a little taut around the edges. 'Luck is a luxury that normally comes along as a result of hard work.'

She glanced down into her wine. 'But sometimes, no matter how hard you try, fate has other ideas for you.'

His eyes narrowed into sharp laser-like beams. 'Yes. But the answer is to turn it to your advantage.'

'Or you can walk away. Find a different option?'

One corner of his mouth lifted. 'Walking away has never been my style.'

She slowly nodded. 'You wouldn't have won championships if you were a man who walked away.'

His expression morphed into something that resembled gratitude. She couldn't claim she understood all his motives but she was beginning to grasp what made Theo tick. As long as he could see a problem in any area of his life, he would not walk away until it was resolved. It was why he was the troubleshooter for Pantelides Inc.

She'd watched footage of him rowing. His grit and determination had held her enthralled throughout the feature and she would be lying now if she didn't admit it was a huge turn-on.

'But there's also strength in walking away. You walked away from rowing rather than risk partnering up with the wrong person.'

He stiffened. 'Inez…'

She fought the urge to back down. 'I don't want to mess up our truce but I want you to just think about it. There's no shame in forgiving. No shame in letting the past *stay* in the past.'

His eyes grew dark and haunted. 'What about my demons?'

'Do you have a cast-iron guarantee that they will be vanquished by the path you've chosen?'

He frowned for several seconds before his eyes narrowed. 'You're right. Let's not mess up the truce, shall we?'

'Theo…'

'*Anjo.* Enough. Have some more wine.' He smiled.

And, just like that, her pulse surged faster. Hell, everything he did made her pulse race. She took a sip and licked her lips as the languorous effect of the wine and the captivating man sitting opposite her took hold.

She really needed to stop drinking so much. She pulled her gaze from the rugged perfection of his face as Camila returned to offer them coffee.

Inez declined and looked over to see his eyes riveted on her.

'I think we need to get you back to the boat.'

Laughter that seemed to be coming easier around him escaped her throat. 'You make me sound as if I've been naughty,' she said after Camila collected their empty plates and left.

'Trust me, I would tell you if you'd been.'

'Well, the night is still young and I'm not ruling anything out.' She laughed again.

His mouth curved in one of those devastating smiles as he reached for his wallet and extracted several crisp notes.

'I say it's definitely time to get you back and into bed.'

Her breath caught. He didn't mean what she thought he meant. Of course he didn't. But images suddenly bombarded her brain that had her blushing.

As she said goodbye to Camila and headed outside, she prayed he wouldn't see her reaction to his words.

'Hey, slow down, you'll break your ankle rushing in those heels.' He caught up with her outside and slid a hand around her waist.

The warmth of his body was suddenly too much to bear. 'It's okay, I'm fine.' Her voice emerged a touch too forceful and he glanced sharply at her.

'What's wrong?'

She raked an exasperated hand through her hair and tried to stem the words forming at the back of her mind. They came out anyway. 'You're supposed to be my enemy. And yet you brought me to one of my favourite places in the world. You're being so kind and attentive and I can't help… I…I want you.'

The transformation that occurred sent her senses reeling. From the charming, desirous dinner companion, Theo turned into a hungry predatory beast in the space of a heartbeat.

He pulled her into a dark alley between two high-rises. Her heart hammered as he held her against the wall and leaned in close.

'You don't want to say things like that to me right now, Inez,' he grated harshly.

His mouth was so tantalising close, she shut her eyes to avoid closing the gap between them and experiencing another potent kiss. 'I don't want to be saying them either. I can't seem to stop myself because it's the truth.'

'That's just the wine talking,' he replied.

She nodded then groaned when he leaned in closer. Heat from his body burned hers and his breath washed over her face. When his stubbled jaw brushed her cheek, she bit hard on her lower lip to stop another groan from escaping.

'Open your eyes, Inez.'

She shook her head. '*Nao…por favor…*'

'What are you begging me for?' he whispered in her ear.

A deep shudder coursed down her spine. 'I don't know…' She stopped and sucked in a desperate breath. 'Kiss me,' she pleaded.

With a dark moan, he touched his mouth to the corner of hers. Fleeting. Feather-light. Barely enough.

Her hands gripped his waist and held on tight. '*Please*,' she whispered.

'*Anjo*, if I start I won't be able to stop. And neither of us wants to spend the night in jail for lewd behaviour.'

She finally opened her eyes. He stood, tall, dark, devastatingly good-looking and tense, with a hunger she'd never seen in a man's eyes. That it was directed at her made her pulse race that much harder.

'Theo.' Her fingers crept up to his face, dying to touch his warm olive skin. 'Let it go. Whatever my father did, revenge would only bring you fleeting satisfaction.'

His jaw tightened but he didn't look as forbidding as he'd looked before. 'It's the only thing I've dreamed about for the last twelve years.'

Her hand crept up to settle over his heart. 'Have you stopped to think that obsessing about it may just be feeding the demons?'

One large hand settled over hers and he stared fiercely down at her. 'Are you offering me another way to quiet them, *anjo*?'

'Maybe.'

He captured her hand and planted a kiss in her palm. When he glanced down at her, a feverish light burned in his molten eyes. 'He doesn't deserve to have you as a daughter.'

'I can say the same about your parents but we play the hand that is dealt us the best way we can. And when it gets really bad I try to remember a happier time. Surely you must have some happy memories with your mother? And was your father really all bad?'

His mouth tightened. Then, slowly, he shook his head. 'No. It wasn't always bad.'

'Tell me.'

He frowned slightly. 'They thought Sakis would be their last child. I came as a surprise, or so my mother tells me. She used to call me her special boy. My father...he took me everywhere with him. He had a sports car—an Aston Martin—that I loved riding in. We'd take long drives along the coast...' He stopped and his eyes glazed over.

She kept silent, letting him relive the memories, hoping that he would find a way to soften the hard ache inside him. But when his eyes refocused, she saw the raw pain reflected in them.

'I'm not a father, and I probably never will be. But even I know those things are easy to do when life's a smooth sail. The true test comes when things get rough. I find it hard to believe that my brothers and I were ever in any way special to our parents when they turned their backs on us when we needed them most. He could've saved me, Inez—' He stopped abruptly and her heart clenched with pain for him.

'How?'

'One simple phone call to warn me and I wouldn't be here…I wouldn't be afraid of going to sleep each night because of hellish nightmares…' A deep shudder raked his tall frame.

'Oh, Theo,' she murmured. He leaned into the hand she placed on his cheek for several seconds then he pulled away and tilted her chin up.

The vulnerable man was gone. 'This changes nothing. I am what I am. Do you still want me?'

She swallowed. 'Yes.'

Something resembling relief swept through his eyes. 'You have half an hour and a lot of head-clearing air before we're back on the boat. I suggest you use that time to think carefully about whether you want this to go any further. Because, once we cross the line, there won't be any going back.'

CHAPTER TEN

THEO THREW THE reins of the launch to the waiting crew member and turned to help her out. Her bare feet hit the landing pad and she swayed a little when the boat rocked.

Contrary to her thinking he would rush her back to the boat after his pronouncement, Theo had taken his time walking her back down the streets to the promenade and onto the beach that led to the pier.

Hell, he'd even taken the time to help her out of her shoes so they could walk along the shore.

But the plaguing doubt that perhaps he didn't want her as much as her screaming senses craved him evaporated the moment she looked into his eyes.

Burnt a dark gold by volcanic desire, he stared down at her for several seconds before he demanded in a hoarse voice, 'Well?'

She licked her lips and watched his agitated exhalation. 'I still want you.'

'Are you sure? There will be no room for regret in the morning, Inez. I won't allow it.'

'I'm not drunk, Theo. Besides, I wanted you this morning and I wasn't drunk then. Or last week, or the first night we met.'

His nostrils flared as he dragged her close on the deserted lower deck. 'That first night, you felt what I felt?'

An impossible attraction that had no rhyme or reason? 'Yes,' she answered simply.

He swung her up in his arms and strode into the galley and down the steps into his large, opulent suite. Somewhere along the line, her shoes fell from her useless hands. She knew they had because her fingers were buried in his hair, and her mouth was on his by the time he kicked the door shut behind them.

Their tongues slid erotically against each other as they explored one another, his forceful, hers growing bolder by the second. Because she knew he liked it, she nipped his bottom lip with her teeth.

His deep growl echoed inside her before he pulled away. Eyes on hers, he slowly lowered her body down his sleek length. Hard muscles and firm thighs registered against her heated skin and even after her feet hit the plush carpet she held onto him, fearful she'd dissolve into a pool of need the moment she let go.

'I need to undress you,' he said raggedly.

Unable to look away from him, she nodded. The dark purple knee-length dress was form-fitting and secured by a side zip. After a couple of minutes of frustrated searching, she laughed and pointed to the hidden zip beneath her arm.

With a dark curse, he lowered it and tugged the dress over her head.

He dropped the dress. He swallowed. Then he stared so hard she stopped breathing.

'*Thee mou*, you're so beautiful,' he groaned.

The feeling suffusing her was different from her reaction to the incandescent hunger in his eyes. It was pleasure that she liked what he saw, that he might well pardon her for her inexperience.

Eager to experience more of the feeling, she reached for her bra clasp.

'No,' he commanded. He grabbed her hands and placed them on his chest. 'That's my job. *You* don't move.'

He drifted his fingers up her sides, eliciting a deep shiver that brought a satisfied smile to his lips. Her bra came undone a second later and he glanced down at her heavy breasts.

'Do you know how long I've waited to taste these?' He cupped one globe in his hand, lowered his head and flicked his wet tongue repeatedly over her nipple.

Fire scorched through her veins and her head fell back as pleasure surged high.

'Theo,' she gasped as he delivered the same treatment to her other nipple. Caught in the maelstrom of sensation, she wasn't aware her nails were digging into his pecs until he hissed against her skin.

'Take my shirt off, *querida*. I want to feel those nails on my bare skin.'

Fingers trembling, she complied with his demand, pulling the shirt off his broad shoulders and down his arms before giving in to the need to caress his bronzed skin. Heated and satin-smooth, his muscles bunched beneath her touch as she explored him.

But, much too soon, he was pulling her hands away, catching her around the waist and striding to the bed.

Depositing her in the middle of the king-sized bed, he stood staring down at her, one hand on his belt. The power and girth of him knocked the breath out of her lungs and a momentary unease sliced across her pleasure.

So far, Theo hadn't commented on her inexperience but the evidence would become glaringly apparent in a few minutes. She opened her mouth to tell him but he was crawling over the bed towards her, his intense focus paralysing her to everything but the pleasure his eyes promised.

He kissed her again, deeper, more forceful than all the times before. She gave in to her need and buried her hands in his hair, scraped her nails along his scalp and won herself a deep groan of pleasure from him. His lips moved along her jaw to nip her earlobe before going lower to explore her neck and lower.

Once again, he suckled her breasts and once again she lost the ability to think straight.

'You love that, don't you?' he observed huskily when he raised his head.

'*Sim*,' she groaned.

'There are many more pleasures, *anjo*. So many more.'

His lips trailed down her midriff…he kissed his way to the top of her panties before he gripped the flimsy material in his hands. Expecting them to be ripped off—a notion that made her wildly breathless—she was surprised when he slowly and gently lowered them down her legs and drew them off.

Equally slowly, taking his time to savour her, he kissed her from ankle to inner thigh. When his mouth skated over her secret place, her hips arched off the bed in delirious anticipation.

She'd never imagined she'd want a man to go down on her but now she couldn't imagine *not* feeling Theo's mouth on her heated core.

At the touch of his mouth, she cried out, her body twisting as pleasure scythed through her. He tasted her so very thoroughly, his tongue, teeth and lips working in perfect harmony to drive her straight out her mind.

She slid ever closer to breaking point, both fearing and yearning for what lay ahead.

Theo slipped his hands beneath her bottom and pulled her even closer to his seeking mouth. With quick expert flicks of his tongue, he sent her careening over the edge.

Her scream was an alien sound, hoarse and pleasure-ravaged, her grip on the sheets tight as she was buffeted by blissful sensation.

He continued to kiss her until she calmed, then kissed his way up her body to seal her mouth with his.

The earthy taste of her surrender seemed to trigger an even more primitive reaction in him. By the time he lifted his head, his eyes were almost black with hunger.

'Did Blanco make you feel like this?' he grated.

She shook her head. 'No.'

Satisfaction gleamed in his eyes. 'By the time I finish making you mine, you will not remember anyone else who came before me.'

Knowing he would discover her inexperience in a matter of minutes, she took a sustaining breath and blurted, 'I never slept with Constantine. Theo, I'm a virgin.'

He froze in the act of reaching for a condom. Several expressions raced over his face before he spoke. 'So I'm to be your first lover?'

She gave a jerky nod. 'Yes.'

Theo absorbed the news and tried to weigh which was the greater emotion swirling through him—shock or elation. The shock was understandable. But the elation, the fact that he was *pleased* he was to be her first? It'd never crossed his mind that she would be a virgin. But suddenly a few things fell into place. Her blushes, her furtive innocent looks, her surprise at his demanding kisses.

Another feeling rose to curl itself around his chest. Possessiveness.

The fact that he was to be her first made him want to beat his chest like a wild jungle animal. He ripped the condom packet open and stared down at her.

The look of apprehension forced him to slow down. He was moving too fast, possibly scaring her. Time to turn it down a notch.

'I'll go as slow as you want, *querida*, but I won't stop,' he warned. He couldn't. He'd come too far. He wanted her too much.

I would've kept you... Perhaps even for ever.

His own words echoed in his head and yet another emotion swept over him. If they'd met in another time, would she be the one? The idea of Inez as his wife, the mother of his children if he'd been normal, washed over him. His heart raced as he stared down at her, so beautiful, so giving.

Thee mou, what the hell was he doing wishing for the impossible? He wasn't normal...

'I don't want you to stop,' she replied. Then she performed one of those actions that illuminated her inexperience. Her gaze flicked down to his groin and she bit her lip. She had no idea how hot that little gesture made him.

A groan ripped from his chest and effectively wiped away the useless yearning.

Planting his hands on either side of her, he parted her thighs with his and settled himself at her entrance.

'Hold onto me, and feel free to dig your nails into my back if it all gets too much.' He attempted a smile and felt a touch of relief when she returned it.

The seductive bow of her mouth called to him and, leaning down, he drove his tongue between her lips. Gratifyingly, she opened up to him immediately. He deepened the kiss and swallowed her groan.

Carefully, he nudged her entrance, fed himself slowly into her wet heat.

He froze as she tensed. 'Easy, *anjo*. Relax,' he murmured soothingly against her mouth.

With a rough little sound she complied. Except now the tension was channelled into him. The feel of her closing around him threatened to tear him apart. Lying in the cradle of her hips, a sense of wonderment stole over him he'd never felt before. And he wasn't afraid to admit it scared the hell out of him.

'Theo.' She said his name with a touch of imploration and frustration that ramped up his tension. Never had he wanted to make it more right for a sexual partner.

He pushed deeper and felt the resistance of her innocence. Those nails dug in. Pleasure roared through him as he pulled back and looked into her beguiling face.

A face that held a touch of apprehension and breathless anticipation.

'Please, Theo. I want you.'

Her husky entreaty was the final straw. With a hoarsely muttered apology, he breached the flimsy barrier and buried himself deep inside her.

She made a sound of pain that pierced his heart then her head was rolling back on a long moan that echoed around the room. He waited until she had adjusted to him. Then he pulled out and rocked back in.

'*Meu deus*,' she voiced her wonder.

'Inez…' he waited until her glazed eyes focused on him, then he repeated the move '…tell me how you feel.'

'*Fantastico*,' she groaned, and Theo was sure she didn't realise she spoke her native tongue.

Her fingers spiked into his hair and when he thrust into her, she met him with a bold thrust of her own. His breath hissed out.

'You're a fast learner, *querida*.' He increased the tempo and gritted his teeth for control when she immediately matched his pace.

All too soon her back arched off the bed, her chest rising and falling in agitation as she neared her climax. Hot internal muscles rippled along his length and he shut his eyes for one split second to rein in his failing grip on reality. Leaning lower, he took one tight nipple and rolled it in his mouth. Her cry of pleasure was music to his ears. He treated its twin to the same attention then lowered himself on her. Sliding his arms under her shoulders he brought her flush against him and thrust in fast, deep movements.

She screamed once before her teeth closed over the skin on his shoulder. Deep shudders rocked through her as her bliss pulled her completely under.

She bit him harder, her nails scouring his back as she rode the unending wave.

When her head fell back towards the pillow, he raised his

head and looked at her face. The expression of wonder and ecstasy sheening her eyes finally sent him over the edge.

With a roar torn from deep inside him, he gave into the shattering release.

He clamped his mouth shut as new, confusing words threatened to burst free. Praise? Gratitude? Hell, *adoration*? When had he ever felt those emotions in connection to a woman he'd just bedded?

He buried his face in her neck and let the ripples of pleasure wash him away in silence. Until he could fathom just what the hell was going on beyond the chemical level with Inez, he intended to keep his mouth shut.

Inez slowly caressed her hands down his back, not minding at all that she was pinned to the bed by his heavy, muscled weight. Right at that moment, she couldn't think of a better way to suffocate to death. The thought made her giggle.

Theo turned his head and nuzzled her cheek. 'Not the reaction I expect after a mind-blowing orgasm but at least it's a happy sound.'

Immediately her mind turned to the dozens of women he'd pleasured before her. Hot green jealousy burned through her euphoric haze and her hands stilled.

'Hey, what did I say?' His voice rumbled through her. When she didn't immediately answer, he raised his head and stared down at her. 'Inez?'

'It's nothing important,' she replied. And it wasn't.

Earlier this evening, she'd tried to make him see a different way. But he'd refused. This thing between them would last until his vendetta with her father was satisfied. She had no business thinking about what women had come before her or who would replace her once he was done with her family and with Rio.

She endured his intent gaze until he nodded and rose. The feeling of him pulling out of her created a further emptiness inside that made her heart lurch wildly.

Deus, she needed to get a grip. Her hormones were a little askew because she had experienced her first sexual act. No need to descend into full melt-down mode.

She watched him leave the bed, his body in part shadow in the lamp-lit room. He entered the bathroom and returned a minute later with a damp towel. When she realised his intention, she surged up and tried to reach for the towel.

'No,' he murmured softly. 'Lie back.'

Her face heating up, she slowly subsided against the pillows and allowed him to wash her.

Incredibly, the hunger returned as he gently saw to her needs and when he finally glanced back at her his nostrils were flared, a sign she'd come to recognise as a control-gathering technique.

Her nipples puckered and her body began to react to the look on his face.

'You need time to recover.'

Her body refuted that but her head knew she needed to take time to regroup. When she nodded, he looked almost disappointed. He returned the towel to the bathroom but left the light on as he came back to bed. Getting into bed, he pulled the covers over their bodies and pulled her into his arms.

She settled her hand over his chest and felt his steady heartbeat beneath her fingers. They lay there in silence until another giggle broke free from her jumbled thoughts.

'I'm beginning to get a complex, *anjo*.' He brushed his lips over her forehead.

'I believe this is the part where we make small talk after sex but I can't come up with a single subject.'

She felt his smile against her temple. 'Wrong. Normally this would be the part when I either leave or do what I just did to you all over again.'

Her heart caught. 'And?'

'I'm trying to rein in my primal instincts and not flatten you on your back again.'

Feeling bolder than was wise, Inez opened her mouth to tell him that he needn't hold it back for much longer. Instead a wide yawn took her unawares.

It was his turn to laugh. 'I think the decision on small talk has been shelved in favour of sleep.' He turned her face up to his and pressed his mouth to hers. Within seconds the kiss threatened to combust into something else. He pulled back with a groan and tucked her against him. 'Sleep, Inez. Now,' he commanded gruffly.

With a secretly pleased smile, she slid her arm around his waist, already feeling the drowsy lure of sleep encroaching.

She woke to moonlight streaming through the windows. The bedside lamp glowed and she judged that she'd been asleep for a few hours.

Beside her, Theo lay on his side, tufts of sleep-ruffled hair thrown over his forehead. In the soft lighting he looked younger and peaceful but still so damn sexy her breath caught just looking at him.

She suddenly needed to commit his likeness to paper. Her pad was next door in her suite. Slowly extracting herself from the arm he'd thrown over her, she pulled on his shirt and went to retrieve it.

Returning just as quietly, she settled herself cross-legged at the foot of the bed and began to draw. Every now and then she paused and took a breath, unable to fathom the circumstances she found herself in.

She was in bed with a man who was bent on destroying her family. And yet the overwhelming guilt she expected to feel was missing. Instead she yearned to save him from the demons that she'd glimpsed in his eyes when he spoke of his nightmares.

She swallowed as a well of sadness built inside her. Despite his outward show of invincibility she'd seen his battle. A battle he believed only revenge would win for him...

She froze as Theo made a sound. It was somewhere between a moan of pain and the bark of anger. His hand jerked out and then closed into a tight fist.

His whole body tensed for a breathless second before his chest started to rise and fall in agitated pants.

She dropped the sketchpad. 'Theo?'

'*No. No! No! Thee mou, no!*' The words were hoarse pleas, soaked with naked fear.

Both hands shot out in a bracing position and his head twisted from side to side.

'Theo!' She rose to her knees, unsure of what to do.

'No. Stop! *Arghh!*' With a forceful lunge, he jolted upright with a blood-curdling cry. Sweat poured down his face and he sucked in huge gulping breaths.

'*Deus*, are you okay?' The question was hopelessly inadequate but it was all she could manage at that moment. Because her heart was turning over with pain for what she'd just witnessed him go through.

She reached out and he jerked back away from her. 'Don't touch me!'

'Theo, it's me. Inez.' Tentatively, she reached out and touched his arm.

He shuddered violently and lurched away from her, staring blankly at her for several seconds before his face grew taut and haunted.

'Inez,' he said with a dark snarl. 'I fell asleep?' There was self-loathing in the question, as if he hated himself for having lowered his guard enough to let the demons in.

Her stomach flipped and her fingers curled into her palm. 'Yes. You…you had a nightmare.'

His mouth twisted with a cruel grimace. 'No kidding. What the hell are you doing here?' he snapped, looking around the room with unfocused eyes.

She frowned. 'We…um, we fell asleep together after…' She stopped as heat rushed up her face.

He turned back to her and his gaze slowly travelled over her. He brushed the hair out of his eyes and gradually the dull green lightened into golden hazel. 'We had sex. I remember now.'

She flinched and watched him with wary eyes.

With sure, predatory moves, he lifted the tangled sheet off his body and prowled to where she was poised on her knees. He stopped a hairsbreadth from her.

'Can I...can I touch you?' she asked, unwilling to have him pull away from her, but a part of her longed to soothe the turbulent blackness in his eyes.

His mouth pinched and he took several steadying breaths before he spoke. 'You want to comfort me?'

'If you'll let me.'

Another deep shudder and he closed his eyes. His head lowered until his forehead rested between her breasts. His arms closed around her and tightened so hard she couldn't move. They stayed like that until his breathing steadied.

'Theo?'

'Hmm?'

'Tell me about your dream.'

He tensed immediately and she bit her lip. He raised his head and stared at her.

'Take my shirt off,' he commanded, his voice hardly above a tortured whisper.

Concern spiked through, despite the heat his words generated. 'Theo, you just had a nightmare—'

'One I want to forget.' His hands were on the back of her thighs, hard and demanding as they caressed up to her bottom. He cupped the globes with more roughness than before but there was no pain in the caress. 'Inez, if you want to help me, do it.'

She drew the shirt over her head and dropped it. His eyes devoured her breasts and his tongue darted out to rest against his bottom lip.

Between her legs, liquid heat dampened her folds and he groaned in dark appreciation as his seeking fingers found her core.

'So ready. So tight,' he rasped. With almost effortless ease, he picked her up, pivoted off the bed and sat on the side. Grabbing a condom, he slipped it on and positioned her legs on either side of him.

'You will *make* me forget.' The words were almost a plea but with a promise of things to come. 'Yes?'

Before she could do so much as nod, he pressed her down on top of him. She cried out as he filled her with his hot, heavy length. His hard grip on her hips controlled the rhythm, which grew more frantic with each thrust.

'Theo,' she gasped as pleasure scalded her insides and rushed her towards ecstasy.

'Shh, no talking,' he instructed.

Biting her lip, she stared into his face.

Torment, anger, pleasure and more than a dose of anxiety mingled into an oddly fascinating tableau. He was still caught up in the hell of his nightmare and her heart broke over his anguish.

She tried to catch his gaze, to transmit a different sort of comfort from the carnal that he clearly sought but he avoided her eyes. Instead he buried his face between her breasts and mercilessly teased her nipples until she whimpered at the torture.

He increased his thrusts, bouncing her on top of him with almost superhuman strength that had her reeling.

Her orgasm crashed into her, flattening her under its fierce onslaught before proceeding to completely drown her.

Through the thunderous rush in her ears, she heard his guttural roar as he achieved his own ruthless release.

Sweat slicked their skin and their breaths rushed in and out in frantic pants. This time, though, there were no pleasurable caresses and giggling was the last thing she felt like doing.

With lithe grace, he twisted around and deposited her on the bed. Without speaking, he strode into the bathroom.

Inez lay on the bed, grappling with what had just happened. In the last twenty-four hours she'd glimpsed the man tortured by his nightmares, had seen a side to Theo she was certain very few people saw. Instead of guarding her own heart, she wanted to open herself up even more to him, find a way of taking away his pain and torment.

Had she not learnt her lesson with Constantine?

No, Theo was nothing like that man who'd taken delight in humiliating her. The retraction Theo had promised had appeared in the online evening edition of the newspaper and she was sure she'd seen a look of contrition in his eyes when he'd watched her read it.

Darkness and light.

She was deeply, almost irreversibly attracted to both. Again her heart twisted and she looked towards the bathroom.

A crash came a second later, followed by a pithy curse. She was off the bed and running into the bathroom before she could think twice.

'I'm fine!' he ground out.

She hesitated in the doorway and watched him. His fingers were curled around the marble sink and his head was bent forward. 'What's wrong, Theo?'

'Dammit, woman, I'm not made of glass. And I've been grappling with my nightmares long before you came along, so leave me alone!'

Hurt shredded her inside. 'Don't push me away.'

He locked eyes with her in the mirror and sighed. 'You're too stubborn for your own good, you know that?'

'Maybe, but before you throw me out I need the bathroom,' she lied.

'Fine; it's all yours.'

He started to turn. That was when she saw his scars. '*Meu deus*, what happened to you?' she whispered raggedly.

His glance ripped from her face to where she pointed to his left hip. The marks were puckered and too evenly spaced and shaped to be an accident. But still her mind couldn't grasp the idea that someone had deliberately inflicted pain on him.

'You mean you haven't guessed already, *querida*? *Your father* happened.'

CHAPTER ELEVEN

INEZ STAGGERED BACKWARDS until her legs hit the vanity unit and she collapsed onto it. 'I don't…you're saying my *father* did this to you?' She shook her head in fierce disbelief.

Theo's mouth twisted. 'Not personally, no. He hired thugs to do it.'

She felt the blood drain from her head. Had she not been seated, she would've swayed under the unbelievable accusation.

'But…why?'

He grabbed a towel and secured it around his waist. 'You did your research on my family. You know what happened to my father.'

She nodded. 'He was indicted for fraud, bribery and embezzlement.'

'Among other things. He was also involved with some extremely shady people.'

He turned and strode from the bathroom.

She followed him, the fear she'd harboured for a long time blooming in her chest. 'And my father was one of these shady people?'

Theo turned and watched her. Shocked knowledge flared in her eyes. For a brief moment, he sympathised with what she was going through. Having the truth blown up in front of you wasn't easy.

In his deepest, darkest moments he still couldn't believe how painfully raw he felt at his father's abandonment.

'My father owed him a lot of money on some crooked scheme they were working on when he was arrested and all our assets were frozen. Your father took exception to being out of pocket. When he realised he wouldn't be paid, he decided to pursue a different route.'

Her haunted eyes dropped to the scars covered by the towel and quickly looked away.

'So I'm here to pay for my father's sins,' she whispered raggedly.

That had initially been his plan. Somewhere along the line that particular plan had become questionable. But he'd be damned before he'd admit that.

'Your father made me pay for my father's. Money and power were his bottom line, and he wanted payback. Nothing else mattered to him, not even the tortured screams of a frightened boy...'

He compressed his lips as her mouth dropped open and anguish creased her face. 'How old were you?'

He raked a hand through his hair. Even as a voice shrieked in his head to stop baring his raw wounds, he was opening his mouth.

'I was seventeen. I was returning from a night out with friends when his goons grabbed me. He had me smuggled from Athens to Spain and threw me into a hole on some abandoned farm in Madrid. Ari found me there two weeks after I was taken. After he damned near bled every single cent he could find from every relative and casual acquaintance in order to stump up the two million dollars ransom that your father demanded.'

Her hands flew to her head, her fingers spiking through the long tresses to grip them in a convulsive stranglehold. 'Please tell me when you say a *hole*...you don't mean that *literally*?' The words were a desperate plea, as if she didn't want to believe how real the monster that was her father.

His smile cracked his lips. 'Oh, yes, *anjo*. A twelve-foot-deep *literal* hole in the ground with vertical sides and no hand or footholds. No light. No heat. One meal a day with a bucket for my necessaries.'

'No…'

'*Yes!* And you know what his men did for *fun* when they were bored?'

She shook her head wildly, her eyes wide and horror-struck as he loosened the towel from around his waist and exposed his puckered skin. 'Cigar tattoos, they called them.'

Tears welled in her eyes and fell down her cheeks. Still shaking her head, she walked to the bed and sank down on it. She buried her face in her hands and a gut-wrenching sob ripped from her throat. After the first one, they came thick and fast.

His chest tightened with emotions he was very loath to name. Each sob caught him on the raw, until he couldn't bear to hear another one.

'Inez! Stop crying,' he instructed hoarsely after five minutes.

She shook her head and sniffled some more.

'Stop it or I'll throw you overboard and you can swim to shore.'

That got her attention. She brushed her hands across her cheeks and speared him with wide, imploring eyes.

'If the only people you saw were his men, how did you know it was my father?'

He couldn't fault her for trying to find a different reality to the one he'd smashed her world with. Hell, he'd done that for a long time after his father had been indicted. 'I followed the money.'

She frowned. 'What?'

'I traced the ransom my brother paid through dummy corporations and offshore accounts. It took a few years but I finally found where it ended up.'

'In my father's account?'

'Yes. And since then I've made it my business to find out how every single cent was spent.'

Her shoulders slumped and tears welled again. He could tell the ground had well and truly shifted beneath her feet.

After several seconds, she raised her head.

'Okay. I'll do whatever you want. For however long you want.'

It was his turn to feel the ground shift under his feet. Shock slammed through him as he realised just how much he wanted to take her. To hang onto her.

But not for the sake of revenge. For an altogether different reason; because he wanted her. Not for her father but *for her*.

He shook his head. 'Inez…'

'I can never buy back those two weeks that were taken from you or the horror you've had to live with. But I can try and find a way to make up for what was done to you.'

'How? By giving me your body whenever and wherever I ask for it?'

She paled a little. But the brave, spirited woman he'd come to see underneath all that false gloss raised her chin. 'If that's what you want.'

His mouth twisted. 'I don't want a damned sacrificial lamb. And I sure as hell don't want you throwing yourself on your sword for that bastard's sake!'

'Then what do you want? You have his company. His campaign is falling apart. He will be left with nothing by the time you're done with him. How much more suffering do you need before you let go of this anger? When will you feel pacified?'

Theo started to answer, then realised he had no answer. The satisfaction he'd thought he'd feel was hollowly absent, as was the deep-seated sense of triumph he'd always thought he would feel when this moment came.

Looking into her face, he saw the pain and confusion reflected there and his puzzlement increased. The ground was still tilting beneath his feet but he'd been on this path for too long to let go.

Hadn't he?

He forced his gaze to meet hers.

'I will let you know when I'm adequately appeased.'

Over the next week, she watched as he slowly dismantled her father's campaign piece by piece. Allegations of impropriety surfaced, triggering an investigation. Although nothing was found to indict Benedicto, his credibility suffered a death blow and any meaningful points he'd managed to retain in the polls dropped to nothing.

On the Monday morning after returning from their sailing trip, the calls to her cell phone started. Both her father and Pietro bombarded her with messages and texts, demanding to know what was going on.

She hadn't needed Theo to warn her not to take their calls. After his revelation, each time she saw her father's name pop up on her screen, her stomach churned with pain and disgust.

Although she'd long suspected that her father's business dealings weren't as pure as the driven snow, she'd never in her wildest dreams entertained the idea that he would condone the brutality that Theo had described. Each time she saw his scars—and she'd seen them every night since their return, when he'd moved her into his suite—a merciless vice had squeezed her heart.

And that vice had tightened every time he'd cried out in the middle of the night after another nightmare.

She'd been surprised that first night after their return when he'd pulled her close after a fiery lovemaking and instructed her to go to sleep.

When he kept her with him the following night, she'd boldly asked him why.

'I don't want to be alone,' he'd stated baldly. And each time he'd come awake he'd reached for her, wrapping his trembling body around her and holding on tight until his nightmare receded and his breathing returned to normal.

More and more, her foolish heart had begun to believe that her presence was making the nightmares, if not any less horrific, then at least tolerable.

Or she could just be living in a fantasy land where her mind and heart had no idea what language the other was speaking. Because she was beginning to believe that her heart was more involved in Theo's welfare than was wise. And yet she couldn't control it enough to make it stop wrenching in pain when he suffered another nightmare, or soar with joy when he took her to the heights of ecstasy. Even the knowledge that some time in the very near future, after his goal to destroy her father was achieved, Theo would pack up his bags and leave Rio for good, made her heart ache in a way that was almost a physical pain.

Santa Maria, she was losing her mind—

'There you are. Teresa told me you're still here. I thought you'd be at the centre by now.' She'd shared more details of her volunteer work with him during the times when he'd been *Normal Theo*, not *Revenge Theo*. And she'd been ridiculously thrilled when he hadn't been judgemental or condescending.

She looked up as he entered the living room and crossed to where she sat, applying finishing touches to the sketch she'd been working on since breakfast an hour ago. She'd thought he'd left for the day but obviously she'd been mistaken.

Glancing up at his lean, solid frame and gorgeous face, her heart performed that painfully giddy flip again and she glanced away. 'I took a day off. I'm…I'm still thinking of resigning.'

He stilled then dropped to his haunches in front of her. 'Why?'

She struggled to breathe as his scent surrounded her, making her yearn to lean in closer. 'This whole thing with my father has brought unwanted attention to people who are already struggling with life's difficulties. I don't think it's fair on the children.'

A look resembling regret passed through his eyes before he blinked it away. After a full minute, he murmured, 'No, it's not. But you won't resign.'

Her heart caught. 'Why not?'

'Because I won't allow you to give up something you love doing. The publicity about your father will go away. I'll make sure of it.'

She met mesmerising hazel eyes. 'Why are you doing this?'

He shrugged. 'Perhaps I'm beginning to realise that I was mistaken about how much collateral damage I was prepared to accept.'

Collateral damage. She was grappling with that when he spoke again.

'I have something for you.'

She glanced warily at him. 'Beware of Greeks bearing gifts. I'm sure I've read that warning somewhere.'

His smile held a certain chill but was heart-stopping nonetheless. 'For the most part, I'd urge you to heed that warning. But this one is completely harmless.' He pulled something from his back pocket and presented it to her. The look in his eyes made her stomach flip as she glanced from his face to the box.

'What is it?' she asked.

'Open it and see.'

She opened the velvet case and gaped at the platinum-linked, three-tiered diamond choker nestling between the two catches.

'Are you trying to make some sort of *macho* statement?'

He shook his head in confusion. 'Sorry, *anjo,* you've lost me.'

'This is a *choker.* You want everyone to see that you own me?'

He frowned. 'What the hell are you talking about?'

'Why a choker? Why not a simple diamond pendant?'

'I asked my jeweller to send a few pieces. I liked the look of that one. So I chose it. No big deal, no mind games. I thought you'd like it,' he finished tersely.

She bit her lip and wondered if she was reading too much into it. Much like she was reading far too much into her feelings for Theo and what would happen when things ended.

'It's a beautiful piece of jewellery. But frankly it's a bit ostentatious for my taste.' She snapped the box shut and held it out to him. 'Besides, since my role as paparazzi bait is over, I don't see where I would wear something like that.'

His jaw tightened and he pushed the box back at her. 'I was just coming to that. Ari is getting married next weekend. You're coming with me as my plus one.'

She couldn't stop her mouth from gaping open any more than she could stop breathing. 'You want me to drop everything and fly to Greece with you?'

'I'm sure you can work something out with the charity. I'm happy to make a donation to cover your absence if you like.'

'I…'

'And we're not going to Greece. Ari and Perla are getting married at their resort in Bermuda.'

'Different continent, same response.'

His eyes narrowed. 'Do I need to remind you that we're only three weeks into our agreement?'

Her fingers trembled and she threw the box down on the sofa. 'No, you don't need to remind me. Call me foolish, but I thought we were getting beyond that.'

'I'm trying to, Inez.'

'Then ask me nicely. For all you know, I may be busy next weekend and would need to rearrange my plans for you.'

He raised an eyebrow. 'Busy doing what?'

'Splitting the atom. Shaving my legs. Rehearsing to join a

circus troupe. What does it matter? You didn't bother to ask. You only brought me trinkets and ordered me to be ready to fly off to Bermuda.' Her mouth trembled and she firmed it.

'You're angry.'

'You're very observant.'

'Tell me why.'

She laughed. Even to her ears it sounded as if it could've easily cut glass. His eyes narrowed as she shook her head. 'What would be the point?'

'The point would be that I would listen.'

She placed her feet on the carpet and tried to stand. He caught her hips and kept her seated in front of him.

This close she could see the hypnotic gold flecks in his eyes. She wanted to drown in them. Wanted to drown in him. She tried to calm her racing pulse.

His gaze dropped to her mouth, then down to her chest and a different sort of fever took hold of her.

'That necklace—'

'Is just a necklace. I thought I'd give it to you now so you could get an outfit to match for the wedding.'

'And the trip?'

'I need a plus one. I need *you*. And you can hate me if you want but I'm not prepared to leave you here so Benedicto can hound you.'

'I can take care of myself.'

His eyes narrowed. 'I don't doubt that. But can you tell me that he won't view your refusal to take his calls this last week as a betrayal?'

Her heart skittered. 'And you think he'll harm me in some way?'

He glanced meaningfully at her arm, then back to her face. 'Sorry, *anjo*, I'm not prepared to take that chance.'

Darkness and light. Tenderness and ruthlessness. It was what kept her emotions on a knife-edge where this man was concerned.

'Will you come to Bermuda with me? Please?'

She glanced at the velvet box. 'I will. But I'm not wearing that necklace.'

'Fine. We'll find you something else.'

'I don't need anything—' Her argument died on her lips when he picked up her sketchpad. She grabbed at it but he held it out of her reach. 'Theo, hand it over.' She breathed a secret sigh of relief when her panic didn't bleed through her voice.

'You're supposed to be designing me a boat.'

'I'm still working on it. I'll show it to you when it's done.'

His gaze brushed her face and settled on her mouth. The intensity of it made her insides contract. After a minute he handed the pad over and rose. 'I look forward to it. We're dining in tonight. I'm in the mood for an early night.'

He left the room just as silently as he'd entered. She realised her fingers were clamped white around her sketchpad and slowly relaxed them.

She flipped through the pages until she came to the one she'd been drawing. It was one of many featuring Theo asleep. She stared at it, seeing the vulnerability and gentleness in his face that he covered up so efficiently when he was awake. When he was asleep he was all light, no darkness. There was a boyishness about him that she only caught rare glimpses of during the day.

Darkness and light. Unfortunately, her heart refused to be picky about which it preferred because, awake or asleep, Theo had captured her emotions so efficiently she was beginning to fear she was falling in love with him.

The nightmare started the way it always did. A glow of light signalled the men's arrival. Followed by the rope ladder and the heavy descent of thick boots, tree trunk thighs and towering thugs.

Each time he'd fought back. A few times he'd landed blows of his own. But each time they'd eventually overpowered him. The tallest, toughest one, the one who favoured those smelly cigars, always laughed. It was the laughter not the pain that triggered his screams. It was a never-ending grating sound that churned through his gut and tripped his heart rate into overdrive.

He felt the scream build in his throat and readied himself for the roar.

Gentle but firm hands shook him awake.

'Theo...*querido!*'

He kept his eyes shut and reached for her, holding on tight as the images receded. The irony of it wasn't lost on him, the thought of how much he now needed the daughter of the man who was responsible for reducing him to a helpless wreck night after night for the last twelve years.

As he held on to her the thought that had plagued him for several days now took hold. He no longer wanted to pursue this vendetta. Yesterday, he'd found himself requesting that the board vote a different way to what he'd originally planned. They'd been stunned. He'd been twice as stunned.

He'd mentally shrugged and told himself there was no reason to turn his back on a healthy profit but he'd known he'd changed his mind for a different reason.

Benedicto was all but finished.

But ending it now would mean Inez would be free to walk away from him. And the very thought of that made him break out in a cold sweat.

He'd managed to buy himself a little more time by persuading her to come with him to Ari's wedding.

After that...

His insides churned as he lay in the darkness and felt her soft hands soothe him.

He pushed away thoughts he wasn't brave enough yet to truly examine.

'*Querido*, are you awake?' she breathed softly.

His heart flipped and his arms tightened convulsively around her soft, warm body. 'I'm awake, *anjo.*'

'I'm not an angel, Theo.'

'You are.'

'If I were an angel, I'd have the power to banish your nightmares,' she replied in a voice fraught with pain.

It took several seconds to realise she ached for him.

Pulling back, he stared into her face.

'You didn't do this to me, Inez.'

Her eyes clouded. 'I know. But that doesn't mean I don't wish you healed.'

His smile felt skewed. 'There's no cure for me, sweetheart,' he said, although he was beginning to doubt that. Just as he was beginning to think that the answer lay right there in his arms. If only there was a way...

'Are you sure? There's therapy—'

'Tried it. Didn't work,' he replied. When he heard the curtness in his voice he soothed an apologetic hand down her back.

She relaxed against him and he buried his face in her hair and breathed her in.

'What happened?'

'What, with the therapy?'

She nodded.

He slowly opened his eyes and stared into the middle distance. 'They spoke about triggers, breathing techniques and anxiety-detectors. There was mention of electro-shock therapy or good old-fashioned pills. I never went back for a second session.'

Her head snapped up. 'You mean all that was at your first session?'

He smiled and kissed her gaping mouth. 'I believed what was wrong with me couldn't be fixed by therapy.'

'*Believed?*'

He realised what he'd said and his breath caught. Was he grasping at straws where there were none?

'I'm beginning to think things aren't as hopeless for me, *anjo.*'

She paled a little but continued to hold his gaze. Slowly,

she nodded. Her luxuriant hair spilled over her shoulder onto his chest as she stared into his eyes. 'I really hope you find closure one day, Theo.'

Simple, frank words, said from the heart. But they froze his insides as surely and as swiftly as an arctic wind froze water.

Because he was seriously doubting that he would ever find peace without this woman in his arms.

CHAPTER TWELVE

THEY BOARDED THEO'S private jet late the next Friday. The moment they stepped on board, Inez sensed something was wrong.

Theo paced up and down, his agitation growing the closer they got to take-off.

When the pilot came through, Theo sent a piercing glance at him and the man hurried into the cockpit.

'Theo, sit down. You're making your pilot nervous.'

He barked out a short laugh and threw himself into the long sofa opposite her chair. His fingers drummed repeatedly on the armrest. 'Don't worry; he's used to it.'

'Used to what?'

'My aversion to enclosed spaces,' he answered tersely.

'Your claustrophobia.' Her heart squeezed as she watched his fingers grip the armrest and the skin around his mouth pale.

Unbuckling her seat belt, she crossed to the sofa and sat down next to him. A sheen of sweat coated his forehead and when his eyes sought hers she read the anxiety in them. Reaching around him, she secured his seat belt then took care of her own as the plane taxied onto the runway.

Taking the arm closest to hers, she pulled it over her shoulder and settled herself against him. He tugged her close immediately, his breathing harsh and uneven.

She hugged him harder, and when he tilted her face up to his she went willingly.

He kissed her with a desperation that tore through her soul. For long, anxiety-filled minutes, he took what she offered, until the need for air drove them apart.

'You get that we cannot kiss all the way to Bermuda, don't you?' she said, laughing.

'Is that a challenge? Because I bet I can,' he threw back with a heart-stopping smile.

Inez noticed that his breathing was no longer agitated and breathed a sigh of relief.

'No, it's not a challenge.' She rested her head on his shoulder and caressed his hard jaw. 'How do you normally get through flying?'

His jaw tightened for a second before he relaxed. 'Mild sleeping pills before take-off normally does the trick.'

'Why not today?'

'You're here,' he said simply. After a minute, he asked, 'Why are you helping me?'

'I cannot forget that my father did this to you. And no, I'm not offering myself as a sacrificial lamb. But I don't want to see you suffer either. I want to help any way I can.'

The reminder that her father loomed large between them grated more than he wanted to admit. 'For how long?' Theo demanded more harshly than he'd intended.

She stiffened. 'Sorry?'

'Are you counting the days until I set you free?' he pressed.

Her eyelids swooped down, concealing her expression. 'I...we have an agreement—'

'Damn the agreement. If you had a choice now, today, would you stay or would you leave?'

'Theo—'

'Answer the question, Inez.'

'I'd choose to stay...'

The bubble of joy that started to grow inside him burst when he registered her flat tone. 'But?'

'But… this could never go anywhere.'

A sense of helplessness blanketed him. 'Why not? Because I blackmailed you?'

She shook her head. 'No. Because a relationship between us would be impossible.

Theo's vision blurred at her words. He'd pushed her too far. Hung onto his vendetta for too long. His mouth soured with ashen hopelessness. 'I guess we both know where we stand.'

When she moved away, he fought not to pull her back. She stayed close—out of pity? His mouth curled. He told himself he didn't care but the voice in his head mocked him.

He cared, much more than he'd bargained for when he'd forced her to make that stupid choice. The idea of her walking away from him made his insides knot with a pain far greater than he'd ever known.

The plane hit a pocket of turbulence, throwing her against him. When she stayed close, he let her. Forcefully, he reminded himself of one thing.

He'd never meant to keep her for ever.

The Pantelides Bermuda resort was a breathtaking jewel set amid swaying palm trees and sugar-white sand. The sun beat down on them as Theo drove the open-top Jeep towards their villa.

Stunning buildings connected by dark wooden bridges under which the most spectacular water features had been constructed made for a visual masterpiece. All round them bold colour burst free in a heady mix of blues, greens and yellows that begged to be touched.

Their sprawling whitewashed villa featured high ceilings, cool tiled floors and a four-poster bed that dominated the master bedroom.

A tense Theo who hadn't said more than a dozen words

to her since they landed, instructed the porter to place their cases in the master bedroom and tipped the man before walking outside onto the large wooden deck.

'There's a barbecue later this afternoon. Perla thought we might want to rest before then. You can go ahead and rest if you want to. I'll go and catch up with Sakis and Ari.'

He walked away from her and headed out of the door.

The clear indication that she wasn't welcome stung, although why she was surprised was beyond her.

He'd held ajar the possibility of continuing this thing between them and she'd slammed the door shut.

A small part of her was proud she hadn't grasped the suggestion with both hands, while the larger part, the part that had fallen head over heels in love with Theo in spite of all the chaos surrounding them, reeled with heart-wrenching pain at what the future held.

But, as she'd told herself over and over again on the plane as he'd shut his eyes and surprisingly dozed off, she was taking the right steps now to prevent even more heartache later.

Because there was no way Theo would ever reconcile himself to having her as a constant reminder. Certainly not enough to love her.

The reality was that they'd fallen into bed as a result of some crazy chemistry. Chemistry fizzled out. Eventually, the constant reminder that a part of her was responsible for his inner demons and outer scars would grate and rip at whatever remained after the chemistry was gone.

He was better off without her.

Her heart protested loudly at that decision. Ignoring it, she went into the bedroom and lifted her case onto the bed. The cream sheath she'd bought for the wedding needed to be hung out before it creased beyond repair.

Unzipping her case, she opened it and froze. A red velvet box, similar to the black one Theo had presented her with a few days ago lay on top of her clothes.

With shaky hands she picked it up and opened it. The stunning necklace sparkling in the sunlight made her gasp.

The platinum chain had a small loop at one end, with a large teardrop diamond at the other that slipped easily through the hoop. The design was simple and elegant. And so utterly gorgeous she couldn't stop herself from caressing the flawless stone.

Swallowing a lump in her throat at the thoughtfulness behind the necklace, she jumped when a knock came at the door. Thinking it was Theo who'd forgotten to take a key, she opened the door with a smile.

Only to stop when confronted by two stunningly beautiful women, one of whom was heavily pregnant, while the other carried a small baby in her arms.

'Sorry to descend on you like this, only Theo was a bit vague about whether you were actually resting or if you were up for a visit.' The women exchanged glances. 'I've never seen him so scatty, have you?' the pregnant redhead asked the blue-eyed blonde.

'Nope, normally he's quick off the mark with those hopeless one-liners. Today, not so much. Anyway, we thought we'd come on the off-chance that you were *not* resting and say hello…oh, my God, that necklace is gorgeous!' The redhead reached out and traced a manicured forefinger over the diamond.

Then she looked up, noticed Inez's open-mouthed gaze and laughed. 'Sorry, I'm Perla soon-to-be Pantelides. This is Brianna Pantelides, Sakis's wife. And this little heartbreaker is Dimitri.'

'I'm Inez da Costa. I'm a…' she paused, for the first time holding up her relationship with Theo to the harsh light of day and coming up short on explanations '…business associate of Theo's.'

The two women exchanged another glance and she rushed to cover the awkward silence. 'Please, come in.'

Brianna paused. 'Are you sure?'

'*Sim*…yes, I'm sure. I was just unpacking…' she started and noticed Perla's frown.

'Why are you doing that yourself? We have two butlers and three villa staff attached to each residence.'

'I think Theo sent them away,' she said, then bit her lip as Perla's eyebrows shot upward.

'Did he? Ari did that once too, when we first arrived here four months ago. Then we proceeded to have an almighty row.' She smiled at the memory and placed her hand lovingly over her swollen belly.

Brianna laughed and walked to the sofa. Settling herself down, she opened her shirt and adjusted her son for a feed.

Perla sat on the sofa too and they both stared back at her. Their open curiosity made her nape tingle.

'We won't keep you long. I just wanted to run the itinerary by you because, frankly, I don't trust the men with the information. We have a casual dinner tonight, followed by a quick rehearsal. Most of the guests arrive in the morning and the wedding is at three o'clock, okay?'

'Okay.' She ventured a smile and Brianna's eyes widened.

'Gosh, you're stunning! How did you meet Theo again?'

'Brianna!' Perla admonished with a laugh.

'What?'

Inez fiddled with the clasp of the velvet box and pushed down the well of sadness that surged from nowhere. These two women were not only almost family, they were friends too. Whereas her family was in utter chaos and she had no friends to speak of.

She forced another smile. 'He had some business in Rio. I was…am helping him out with it.'

'Right. Okay.' Perla struggled upright and nudged Brianna. 'We'll leave you alone. I think the guys are rowing in about an hour. It's an experience you don't want to miss if you've never seen it before.'

Brianna gently dislodged her drowsy baby from her

breast and laid him on her shoulder, gently patting his back as she stood.

The door opened as they neared it and Theo's large frame filled the doorway.

His gaze zeroed in on her, then dropped to the box still clutched in her hand before coming back up. Her throat dried at the sight of him and the ever present tingle that struck her deep within flared heat outward.

'Um, Theo?' Perla ventured.

'What?' he snapped without taking his eyes from Inez.

'You need to move from the doorway so we can leave.'

He snorted under his breath and entered the villa. He turned with his hand on the door, causing Brianna to roll her eyes. 'We've given Inez the schedule so you have no excuse to be late.'

'I'm never late.'

'Yeah, right. You were almost two hours late for Perla's engagement party and an hour late for Dimitri's christening.'

'Which therefore means I'll only be half an hour late for this wedding. Now, please go and pester your other halves and leave me alone.'

The women grumbled as they left. He turned from the door with a smile on his face but it slowly dimmed as his gaze connected with hers.

'Did they harass you?' he asked, a touch of wary concern in his eyes.

She shook her head. 'No. They were lovely.'

'I don't know about lovely but I tolerate them.' Contrary to his words, his voice held a fondness that made her chest tighten.

Theo understood family. Enough that he'd been devastated when his had been broken. And yet he'd wanted to rip hers apart.

Despite understanding the reason behind his motives, the thought still hurt deeply.

'Inez?'

She turned sharply and headed back to the bedroom. He followed and grabbed her wrist as she reached out to set the box down.

'What's wrong?'

Her throat clogged. 'What *isn't* wrong?'

His eyes narrowed. 'If Brianna or Perla said something to upset you—'

'No, I told you they were wonderful! They were kind and funny and…and incredible.' Tears threatened and she swallowed hard.

'You only met them for twenty minutes.'

'It was enough.'

'Enough for what?'

'Enough to know that I want what they have. And that I'll probably never have it. So far my record has been beyond appalling.'

He frowned. 'You don't have a record.'

'Constantine used me to get dirt on my father and—'

'I don't want you to say his name in my presence,' he interrupted harshly.

'And what about you? You make me hope for things I have no right to hope for, Theo. What sort of fool does that make me?'

'No, you're not a fool. You're one of the bravest, most loyal people I know.' He said the words gravely. 'It is I who is the fool.'

Theo's words echoed through her mind as she watched the brothers row in perfect harmony across the almost still resort water a short while later.

He took the middle position with Sakis in front and Ari at the back. She watched, spellbound, as his shoulders rippled with smooth grace and utmost efficiency.

'Aren't they something to watch?' Perla sighed wistfully.

'*Sim*,' she agreed huskily.

'I think they do that just to get us girls all hot and bothered,' Brianna complained but Inez noticed that she didn't take her eyes off her husband for one second.

When the men eventually returned to shore, the two women joined them and were immediately enfolded into the group.

Theo glanced her way, a touch of irritation in his eyes. Seconds later, he broke away from the group and came towards her.

'I didn't expect you to be down here. You should be resting.'

'I was invited. I hope I'm not intruding.'

'If you were invited then you're not intruding. Come and join us.' He grabbed her hand and led her to where Ari and Sakis were turning over the boat to dry the underside.

The two brothers gave her cursory glances but barely spoke to her. When Ari abruptly asked Theo to accompany him to the boat shed, her stomach fell.

Perla organised a Jeep to take her back to their villa and when Theo returned half an hour later, his jaw was tight and his movements jerky as he swept her off her feet and strode into the bedroom.

He made love to her with a fierce, silent passion that robbed her of speech and breath before he clamped her to his side and slid into sleep.

Her eyes filled with tears and she hurriedly brushed them away. It was no use daydreaming that things would ever magically turn rosy between her and Theo.

As much as she wanted to wish otherwise, they were on a countdown to being over for good.

The wedding was beautiful and quietly elegant in a way only an events organiser extraordinaire like Perla could achieve despite being seven months pregnant. Inez watched the bride and groom dance across the polished floor of the casino, transformed into a spectacular masterpiece that stood directly on the water, and fought the feelings rampaging through her.

Theo would never be hers. She would never have a wedding like this or have him gazing at her the way Ari was gazing at his new wife.

She would never feel the weight of his baby in her belly or have it suckle at her breast.

Despair slowly built inside her, despite knowing deep down that Theo had done her a favour by bringing her here. He didn't need her to save him from whatever nightmares plagued him. He had a family that clearly adored him, who would be there for him when he chose to let them in.

She needed to stop moping and get on with her life.

Her time in Theo's house and his bed was over. In retrospect, she was thankful she'd let him talk her into keeping her volunteer position. It was a lifeline she was grateful for in a world skidding out of control. The things she couldn't control she would learn to live without.

A tall figure danced into her view and her eyes connected with the man who occupied an astonishingly large percentage of her mind. In his arms was an elegantly dressed woman with greying brown hair and a sad expression. She said something to him and he glanced down at her. His smile was gentle but wary and Inez saw her sadness deepen.

Inez heard the soft gurgle of a baby over the music and turned to see Brianna next to her. 'That's their mother.' She nodded to Theo's dance partner. 'Their relationship has been fraught but I think they're all finding their way back to each other.' She glanced at Inez with a smile. 'I hope that you two find your way too.'

Inez shook her head. 'I'm afraid that's impossible.'

Brianna laughed. 'Believe me, I've seen the impossible happen in this family. I've learned not to rule anything out.' She smiled down at her child and danced away with him towards her husband.

Tears stung her eyes as she watched Sakis enfold his wife and son in his arms.

'What's wrong now?' Theo's deep voice sounded in her ear.

She blinked rapidly and pasted a smile on her face. 'Nothing. Weddings…they make me emotional. That's all.'

His eyes narrowed speculatively on her face before he took hold of her elbow. 'Dance with me.'

He led her to the dance floor and pulled her close.

'You have a big family,' she said, more for something to fill the silence.

'They can be a pain in the rear sometimes.'

'Regardless, you all seem to watch out for each other.'

He shrugged. 'Force of habit.'

'No, it's not. Does Ari know who I am?'

His mouth tightened. 'He suspects. I didn't enlighten or deny because it's none of his business. He's welcome to draw his own conclusions. Why do you ask?'

'Because he's been watching me like a hawk since we got here and he hasn't spoken more than two words to me. That's what I mean. What you have with your brothers isn't habit. It's love.'

His mouth twisted in a way that evidenced his dark pain.

'*Love* hasn't conquered the nightmares that have plagued me for all these years, Inez.' The raw pain in his voice made her throat clog. She forced a swallow.

'Because you haven't allowed it to. You resisted any attempt at help because you thought you had to face this demon alone, do things your way.'

The honest barb struck home. He was silent for the rest of the song. Then abruptly he spoke. 'I didn't want to appear weak. I hated myself every time I couldn't walk into a dark room or down an unlit street. I haven't been able to cope with the smell of cigars without breaking out in a cold sweat. Do you know what that feels like?' he asked in a harsh undertone.

She shook her head. 'No, but I know it will never go away if you keep it buried.'

Her warmth, her strength hit him hard and he wanted to reach for her with all he had. Suddenly, everything he'd ever craved, ever wished for seemed coalesced in the woman before him.

'It's no longer buried. A month ago I was still the messed-up boy Ari dug up from that hole twelve years ago. But you did something about that.'

'No, I'm not responsible for that.'

His hand cupped her nape and he whispered fiercely in her ear. 'You are. You've seen me, Inez. I can't sleep with the lights off. I used to panic whenever someone shut a door behind me. That's why I surrounded myself with glass. With you by my side I flew here with no need for sleeping pills.'

'Even though you refused to speak to me for hours.'

He exhaled. 'Things are upside down and inside out right now. Let's just…we'll get through this wedding and head back to Rio. And we will damn well fix this thing between us. Because I'm not prepared to let you go yet.'

CHAPTER THIRTEEN

'I TOLD YOU, you're so much better than a damn sleeping pill.'

Inez laughed as Theo tugged her dress down and lifted her out of it. Leaving it on the floor of the master cabin bedroom, he waited for her to kick her shoes off before he crossed over to the bed. The diamond pendant he'd looked incredibly pleased that she'd worn lay nestled between her breasts.

'Keep that on,' he instructed, just as the plane jerked through turbulence and they fell onto the bed together, a tangle of hard and soft limbs and hot, needy kisses.

'I'm glad I have my uses,' she said, laughing, when he let her up for air.

His face grew serious as he stared down at her. 'You've attained the ultimate purpose in my life, *querida*. Now more than ever you're my saviour: *my* angel.' He cradled her head as he kissed her.

Inez closed her eyes and imagined that she could feel his soul through his reverent kiss. She studiously ignored the voice that mocked that she was deluding herself.

When he finished undressing her with gentle hands, she tried to stem her tears as he made love to her with a greedy passion that touched her very soul.

Afterwards she held him in her arms as he fell asleep. Unable to sleep, her mind drifted back to the wedding.

Theo had introduced her to his mother and again she'd witnessed the sadness in her eyes. When he'd hugged her at the end of the evening and murmured gently into her ear, his mother had burst into tears. Inez had watched as the brothers closed around her and soothed her tears.

She was still watching them when Ari had glanced her way. His measured smile and thoughtful nod in her direction had made her swallow. It hadn't been acceptance but it hadn't been the chilly reception he'd given her either.

As they'd packed to leave, Inez had asked Theo about what had happened with his mother.

'She fell apart completely after my father was arrested. She left Athens and locked herself away at our house in Santorini,' he'd replied in an offhand manner, but Inez had seen his anguish.

Recalling his words about abandonment, she'd gasped, 'She wasn't there when you were kidnapped, was she?'

Heart-shredding pain washed over his face, but a moment later it was replaced by a look even more soul-shaking. Forgiveness. 'No. She wasn't. But I had Ari and Sakis. They were strong for me. And they were that way because of her. I told her that tonight because I think we both needed to hear it.'

His words had resonated deep inside her. But most of all it had been his statement on the dance floor that continued to flash across her mind. *I'm not prepared to let you go yet.*

Her heart lurched. He meant to keep her in his bed for a while yet. Like a trophy he wasn't prepared to relinquish. And her foolish heart performed a giddy little samba at the thought of having a few more moments with him.

She woke to kisses on her forehead and her cheek and opened her eyes to bright sunshine.

'Good, you're awake. We just landed.'

She yawned widely. 'Already? I feel as if I just fell asleep.'

He laughed. 'It's three o'clock in the afternoon. And we have much to do before tonight.'

She stared at his wide grin and her heart lifted with happiness. 'You seem in very good spirits, *querido*,' she commented.

He gathered her close in his arms and gazed down at her. 'There is a reason for that.'

'Tell me,' she murmured softly.

His face turned serious, his eyes fierce as he watched her. 'For the first time in twelve years, I slept through the night without a nightmare,' he muttered hoarsely.

Theo watched her face light up with shocked pleasure before she reached up to clasp his face. Her kiss was gentle and sweet. 'Oh, Theo. I'm so happy for you.'

'I'm happy for *us*,' he replied. With another kiss, he got up and started dressing. 'Get a move on, sweetheart, unless you wish to give the customs guy an eyeful when he boards.'

With a yelp she got up and pulled her clothes on.

Theo's phone started ringing the moment they stepped off the plane. And it wasn't until they were back home that she remembered what he'd said on the plane.

'What did you mean—"we have much to do before to-night"? We're not going out, are we?' She groaned.

He took the phone from his pocket and checked it as another text message came through. She waited impatiently for him to finish.

'No, we're not going out. But we have a guest coming.'

'A guest? Who?'

'I've invited your father to dinner.'

Inez staggered as if a bucket of ice had been poured over her.

'My father is coming here?'

'Yes.'

'And you didn't think to inform me of this? What makes you think I want to see him?'

'We have to. It's time to get this thing over and done with, once and for all.'

'And you don't care how I feel about it?'

'I thought we agreed to fix things when we return to Rio?' he asked with a frown.

'Yes, but when you said *we*, I thought you meant us, you and me. More fool me. Because there is not me without my father, is there?'

'What are you talking about? Of course there is.'

'Then why would you go behind my back to arrange this?'

A tic started in his temple. 'Because it's my fault you're in the middle of all this.' He sighed and clawed a hand through his hair. 'I got a chance to fix things with my mother in Bermuda. We may never get back what we had but I'll take that over nothing. Whatever relationship you choose to have with your own father from here on in is up to you. But this is a hardship I caused in your life and one I have a duty to fix.'

The fight fizzed out of her but the fear that something had gone seriously wrong between the airport and home wouldn't go away.

At seven on the dot, the doorbell rang. She passed her hand over her black jumpsuit and tucked a lock of hair nervously behind her ear as she stood by Theo's side.

The butler entered the living room, followed by her father.

Benedicto da Costa drew to a halt. His narrowed gaze slid from Theo to her, his face a mask of dark anger and cold malice she'd forced herself to overlook in the past.

Now she saw him for who he really was. Images of Theo's scars flashed through her mind and her hands fisted at her side.

'I won't shake your hand because this isn't a social visit,' he rasped icily to Theo. 'And I won't be dining with you, either.'

'Perfectly fine by me. Frankly, the quicker we get this over with the better. But let me remind you that you're here only because of Inez. She may be your daughter but she's under my protection now. I suggest you don't lose sight of that fact. What business you and I have will be finished by week's end.'

Her father's gaze swung back to her. 'Are you just going to stand there and let him speak to your father that way? You disappoint me.'

'That's no surprise. I've been a disappointment from the moment I was born a girl, *Pai*.'

'Your mother will be rolling in her grave at your behaviour.'

She raised her chin. 'No, actually. *Mãe* told me every day she was proud of me. She also encouraged me to follow my dreams. She wanted to be a sculptor. Did you know that?'

'What's your point?'

'She was talented, *Pai*. But she gave it up for you. It was her, not you, who taught me what loyalty and family meant. You were only focused on exploiting that loyalty for your own selfish needs.'

His face tightened and his eyes flickered to Theo, who'd been standing by her with his arms folded, a half smile on his face.

'Is this what I came here for? To be lectured by an ungrateful child?'

Theo shrugged. 'I'm finding it quite entertaining.'

Benedicto growled and shot to his feet. 'If there is a point, *son*, I suggest you get to it.'

Theo grew marble-still, his smile disappearing in the blink of an eye. Pure rage vibrated off his body and Inez watched his nostrils flare as he sucked in a control-sustaining breath.

'*I am not your son.* And you are not worthy to be a father. It's a shame you didn't learn how to be a better parent from the mother who gave birth to you in that *favela* you deny you grew up in. And don't bother denying it again. I know everything there is to know about you, da Costa.'

For the first time since he'd walked in, Benedicto grew

wary. He strolled to the drinks cabinet and took his time examining all the expensive spirits and liqueurs displayed.

Without asking, he poured a measure of single malt whisky and took a bold sip. 'So I bent the truth a little. So what? You've already discredited my campaign. What do you want? My company? Is that your end game? You want to pick up the shares for Da Costa Holdings for peanuts? Well, over my dead body.'

Theo's laugh was menacing enough to cause her skin to tingle in alarm. 'Trust me, a few weeks ago it would've been my pleasure to grant you your wish. But you're wrong on that score. Your company is of no interest to me.'

His wariness increased. 'What's changed?'

Theo's eyes flicked to her and her heart thudded. 'Your daughter.'

'Really?'

Inez shook her head in astonishment. 'Do you really not know who he is, *Pai*?' she asked.

Theo's mouth curved in a mirthless smile. 'Oh, he knows who I am. He's just hoping that *I* don't know what he did twelve years ago.'

Benedicto swallowed, his gaunt face growing pale until he looked ashen. 'I have no idea what you're talking—'

She rushed towards him, anger, pain and disappointment coiling like poisonous snakes inside her. 'Don't you dare deny it. *Don't you dare!*' Her voice cracked and a sob broke through her chest. 'You had a boy kidnapped and tortured! For money. How could you?'

Eyes she'd once thought were like her own turned black with sinister rage. 'How could I? I did it for you. The fancy clothes you strut about in and that fancy car you drive? Where do you think the money came from? I needed it to save the company. Anyway, it was my money. Why did I have to go back to farming just because Pantelides couldn't keep it in his pants or stop his bit on the side from blowing the whistle on him?'

Inez's hand flew to her mouth, her insides icing over. '*Santa Maria*, you truly are a monster.'

Her father's jaw tightened and he addressed Theo. 'Is this the point where you hand whatever file you've gathered on me over to the authorities?'

Theo's mouth twisted. 'So you can bribe your way out of jail? No.'

Benedicto frowned. 'Then what the hell do you want?'

Theo glanced over at her and a look of almost relief washed over his face, as if a weight had been lifted off his shoulders. 'That's up to Inez. And only her. I'm done with you.'

Inez raised her suddenly heavy head and looked from one man to the other.

One stood tall, proud and breathtaking. A man she'd been so determined not to let in. But whose tortured vulnerability had drawn her to him, made her see beneath his skin to the frightened child who was desperately seeking answers.

Choking tears filling her eyes, she turned to the monster who was her father. 'I have nothing else to say to you. I don't want to see you ever again. Goodbye.'

Turning sharply from both men, she rushed out of the room and fled up the stairs.

Theo wasted no time in throwing Benedicto out once Inez left the room. He'd meant what he said—he was done with seeking retribution…had been done almost from the moment he'd met Inez.

Perhaps unwisely, he'd thought the meeting with Benedicto would be swift and cathartic. Instead, he'd brought Inez even more anguish.

He slashed his fingers through his hair as he vaulted up the stairs that led to his third floor suite. Perhaps she'd been right. He'd ambushed her in his rush to get this situation sorted between them.

But he would make it right for her. They would get

through this. They had to. The feelings he'd tried hard to smother had blown up in his face when he'd woken on the plane this afternoon. With the absence of anxiety and fear, the purest reason why he wanted to wake up each morning with Inez had shone through.

The feelings had been so intense he'd almost blurted it out. But he'd decided to wait until she'd confronted her father.

Now he wished he hadn't. He was wishing he'd provided her with that additional support of knowing how much she meant to him before he'd let her father loose on her.

Pursing his mouth in determination, he pushed the bedroom door open. 'Inez, I'm sorry for—'

The sight that confronted him silenced his words and turned his feet to clay. She stared at him, eyes red-rimmed with freshly shed tears.

Because of him. But even that pulse of deep regret couldn't erase the sight before him.

'What are you doing?' he asked, although the part of his brain that hadn't frozen along with his feet could work it out.

Two suitcases were open on the bed, one filled with her clothes. *She was packing...*

The silk top in her hand trembled before she turned and threw it in her case. Then her fingers curled around the edge of the lid.

When she looked at him again, more tears filled her eyes.

'Thank you for opening my eyes to what he truly is,' she murmured huskily.

'Shelve the thanks and tell me what you're doing,' he replied tersely.

One hand swiped at her cheek. 'I'm leaving, Theo.'

'You're what?' His voice rang with disbelief. 'You're going back to your father's house?'

She shuddered from head to toe. 'No. I could never live there again.'

He frowned. 'Then where are you going?'

She gave a tiny shrug. 'I'll stay with Camila.'

He finally got his feet to work and paced to where she stood. When she grabbed her shorts, he ripped them from her hand and threw them on the bed. 'I seem to be missing a link somewhere, sweetheart. Why don't you take a beat and fill me in?'

'I can't stay here.'

A merciless vice squeezed his chest. 'Why not?'

Her face creased in fresh anguish. 'Because he is right. The food he put on our table; the clothes on my back; our fancy education. They *all* came from your suffering.'

'For God's sake—'

She carried on raggedly. 'I never stopped to think about it but I remember the day he came home twelve years ago and told my mother our troubles were over. We weren't exactly poor before then, but after he pressured my mother into selling the ranch he made some bad investments and the company suffered for it. They argued a lot and I used to go to bed every night praying for a miracle just so they'd stop arguing. Can you imagine how I felt when my prayers were answered? And now, all these years later, I find out that what I'd prayed for came at the cost of your—' She choked to a stop, then frantically threw more clothes into the case.

Theo couldn't find an answer as desperately as he tried. He was watching her torture herself and he could do nothing to stop it. '*Anjo*—'

'No. I'm *not* an angel, Theo. I'm a child of the monster, a heartless devil who tortures children and doesn't feel an ounce of regret for it. How can you even bear to look at me?'

'Because you're *not* him!' he interjected fiercely. He took her hands and forced her to face him. 'You're not responsible for his actions. Stay, Inez. We said we would talk about us once we were done with him.'

'But there is no us, is there? We…we just fell into bed because of the circumstances that brought us together. If it hadn't been for my father you'd never have set foot in Brazil.'

'So you're walking away because you think we were never meant to be?' He watched her, forced himself to think how he would feel if she walked away from him. The realisation of what was happening washed over him and ashen despair filled his chest.

'I'm walking away because you need to put everything and everyone associated with your ordeal behind you. Otherwise you will never heal properly.'

He dropped her hand and stared down at her. The ice that had started to build inside him since he'd walked into the room hardened. It crept around his heart and Theo swore he heard it crack. His eyes scoured her beautiful tearstained face, looking for a tiny chink. A tiny ray of hope that would offer deliverance from the quicksand of devastation he could feel himself sinking into.

'So that's it? That's your final decision. You're doing this for my sake but I have no say in the matter?' He couldn't stop the bitterness from lacing his voice.

Her answer was to step back and gather up the last of her clothes. With trembling fingers, she zipped up the cases and lifted them off the bed.

'Inez, answer me!'

She stilled at the door. '*Adeus*, Theo.'

'Go to hell!' he snarled back.

'Table Four need a second helping of *feijoadas*. And a bottle of Rioja.' Camila bustled into the kitchen, checked on the bubbling pot Inez was stirring and nodded in approval. '*Fantastico*. I'll be back in a minute for that order.' She sailed back out on a giddy whirlwind.

Inez wiped her sweating brow and looked over her shoulder. 'Pietro, you grab the bottle; I'll serve up the *feijoadas*.'

Her brother rolled his eyes. 'Who made you queen of the kitchen?'

'I did, when I won the coin toss earlier.'

Her grin came easier today—much easier than it had for far longer than she wanted to dwell on. She still couldn't go for more than ten seconds without thinking of Theo but if she could joke with her brother, that was a good sign that this hollow, half-dead devastation she carried inside her would eventually ease. Right?

'I still think you cheated,' Pietro grumbled.

She lifted one shoulder. 'I'll let you explain to Camila, then, why the Rioja isn't here when she returns, *sim*?'

'Tomorrow, I'm tossing the coin.' He sauntered down the stairs into the basement that served as the restaurant's larder and wine cellar. The smell of the cheese Camila kept in the small space could be overpowering and she smiled again as Pietro made gagging noises.

If there was a bright side to be seen, it was that, amid all the chaos and heartache, somehow she and her brother had grown closer than she'd ever dreamed possible.

They both were yet to decide what they wanted to do with their lives after choosing to walk away from their father and the company, but Camila had encouraged them to take their time. To heal. To reconnect.

When her mother's childhood friend had offered them a job in her restaurant they'd both jumped at it. She'd worked it around her volunteer work and, between the two jobs, it kept her plenty busy.

Keeping herself occupied stopped the tight knot of pain inside her from mushrooming into unbearable agony. In the dark of the night when she lay wide awake and aching was time enough to suffer through the hell of wondering if she was doomed to heartache for ever.

Of wondering if Theo had left Rio in the three weeks since their final bitter encounter. Of wondering if his nightmares were gone for good or if her brief presence in his life had made them worse.

Her hand trembled and she immediately curled it into a fist. Theo was strong. He would survive…

Yes, but he called you his saviour. His angel. And you walked away from him.

'No,' she breathed through the pain ripping through her. She'd done the right thing—

'No what? If you tell me I've got the wrong wine, you'll have to go and get it yourself.'

She shook her head blindly and turned gratefully to the door as Camila walked in. Her quick but assessing glance at her made Inez frown.

'We have a new booking. Table One. And an order of *feijoadas* for one.'

'Wow, you're on fire tonight, sis.'

She ignored Pietro. 'Okay, I'll serve it up and—'

'No, I didn't take a drink order. And I think they want an appetiser first too. Can you go take care of it?'

Inez's eyebrow shot up. 'Me? But I'm not dressed to serve.'

'Pfft. This isn't the Four Seasons, *meu querida*. Besides, it's time you took a break from that hot stove. Tidy your hair a bit and go and take the order.'

Inez looked down at her black skirt and grey T-shirt. It wasn't standard waitress attire but, as Camila had said, this wasn't the Four Seasons. She tucked a strand of hair behind her ear and caught the worried look in the older woman's eyes. It was an expression she'd spied a few times and she reached out and shook her head before the concern could be voiced.

'I'm fine.'

Camila's mouth pursed. 'Good. Then go and attend to Table One.'

With a weary sigh, she washed and dried her hands on her apron. Unfastening it, she hung it on the hook and avoided her image in the small mirror by the door. Her red face from manning the stove for the last three hours would depress her even more.

Plucking a pencil, notebook and menu from the kitchen stand, she nudged the swinging doors with her hip and turned towards Table One.

'You…' she choked out.

Through the drumming in her ears she heard the items in her hand clatter to the floor. A couple of diners glanced her way. Someone picked up the scattered items and placed them in her numb hands. She opened her mouth to thank them but no words emerged.

Every atom in her body was paralysed at the sight of Theo Pantelides.

She heard movement behind her. 'You can't stand here all night, *pequena*. Life will pass you by that way,' Camila said solemnly.

She exhaled shakily and forced herself to move.

Those light hazel eyes never left her as she approached his table. He looked as powerful and as magnificent as ever, even if his cheekbones seemed to stand out a little more than she remembered. His hair had grown a little longer and looked a little dishevelled.

'Sit,' he rasped.

Her heart lurched at the sound of his voice. Licking her dry lips, she shook her head. 'I can't. I'm working.'

'I've received special dispensation from Camila. Sit,' he commanded again.

She sat. He stared at her for a full minute, his eyes raking over her face as if he had been starved of her… Or he was committing her face to memory one last time?

White-hot pain ripped through her. 'Why are you here, Theo?' she blurted.

His eyes rose from her mouth to connect with hers. The breath he took was deep and long. 'I was clearing out the house and I found something you left behind.' He reached down near his feet and laid her sketchpad on the table.

She stared at it, drowning beneath the weight of her despair. 'Oh, thank you.' She paused a second before the words were torn out of her. 'So you're leaving Rio?'

He shrugged. 'There's nothing left for me here.'

Tears burned her eyes as her heart shredded into a million useless pieces. 'I…I wish you well.'

He made a rough sound under his breath. 'Do you?' he asked sarcastically. She glanced up sharply but he wasn't done. 'Problem is, I'd believe those blithe words from the woman sitting across from me. But the woman who drew these…' he flicked over the pages of the sketchpad a few times before he stopped and pointed '…this woman has guts. She was brave enough to draw what was in her heart; what cried out from her soul. Look at her.'

She kept her eyes on his face, her whole body trembling wildly as she gave a jerky shake of her head.

'Look at her, dammit!'

She sucked in a breath. And looked down. The first sketch was the one she'd made of him after they'd made love that first time on the boat. The ones that followed were variations of that first sketch. She'd captured Theo in various poses, each one progressively more lovingly detailed until the final one of him with his brothers, laughing together at the wedding. She'd drawn that from memory on their final night in Bermuda. Staring at the finished picture had cemented her feelings for him.

He turned the page and the image of Brianna and Sakis's baby stared back at her. Dimitri already bore the strong, captivating mark of the Pantelides family. It was that template that she'd used in the following sketches, when capturing her own secret yearning of what her and Theo's baby would look like on paper had been too strong to resist.

'You must think I'm some sort of crazy stalker.'

'There is no stalking involved when the subject is just as crazy about the stalker,' he rasped in a raw undertone.

Her heart flipped into her belly and her whole body trembled. 'You can't be. Theo, I'll ruin your life.'

'I thought my life was ruined before I met you. I was consumed by rage and a thirst for revenge. I let the need for revenge swallow me whole, blinding me to what was important. Family. Love. I thought there was nothing else worth fighting for. But I was wrong. There was you. My life *will* be ruined. But only if you're not in it.'

The tears she'd tried to hold back brimmed and fell down her cheeks. Theo cursed and looked around. 'What's through there?' he asked.

'It's a room, for private parties.'

'Is there a party tonight?'

Before she'd finished shaking her head he was standing and tugging her after him. He kicked the door shut and turned to her.

'Listen to me. You told me I would never see you as anything but the child of a monster. But you forget you're also the child of a loving mother who celebrated every day the special person you are. How do you think she would feel to see you buried here, punishing yourself for what your father did?'

She shut her eyes but the tears squeezed through anyway.

'Open your eyes, Inez.'

She sniffed and complied, staring up at him with blurred vision. 'Now, truly open your eyes and see the wonderful person you are. See the person I see. The brave, talented person who drew those pictures.'

'Oh, Theo,' she cried.

'You have a dream. A dream I want to be a part of.' His hands shook as they traced her face.

'I want that dream to become reality so badly.'

'Then please forgive me for blackmailing you and give us that chance.'

She pulled back. 'Forgive you? There is nothing to forgive. If anything, I should be thanking you for shaking me out of my bleak existence. Even before I truly knew you, you empowered me to fight for what I wanted.'

'So will you fight for us? Will you give me the chance to prove to you that I'm worthy of your love and let me show you how much you mean to me?'

She touched his face and inhaled shakily when he turned to kiss her palm. '*Meu querido,* I fell in love with you so ridiculously soon after meeting you, I swear I'll never confess to you when it happened.'

His stunned laugh brought a wide smile to her face. '*Anjo…*' When her smile dimmed, he shook his head. 'Don't bother to argue with me. I love you with every breath I take. You're my angel and I'll keep repeating it until you believe it.'

'We're not going to have a very smooth-sailing future, are we?'

'No,' he concurred with a laugh then kissed her until her head swam with delirious pleasure. 'But that will be part of our story. And, speaking of smooth sailing…'

'*Sim?*'

'I sent a couple of your sketches to our design guys in Greece. They're interested in talking to you about them. If you're up for it?'

Her mouth dropped open. She waited until he'd kissed it shut before she tried again. '*Really?*'

'Really. And I should bring you good news more often. That happy wriggle does incredible things to my—'

She clamped her hand over his mouth and glanced, alarmed, over his shoulder, just as two text messages beeped in quick succession. He groaned and was about to activate them when a knock sounded on the door.

'*Hell,* I knew I should've found a quieter place for this.'

The door opened and Pietro entered with a bottle of champagne and two glasses.

Theo's expression grew serious as he watched him approach.

Pietro set the bottle and glasses down and stared back at Theo. 'You took care of my sister when I was too much of a *burro* to do so. I'll be for ever in your debt.' He held out his hand.

After several seconds, Theo shook it. 'Don't mention it. Any man who's not afraid to call himself an ass is all right in my book.'

With a self-conscious laugh, Pietro turned to leave.

'Thanks for the drinks,' Theo said. 'But how did you know?'

Inez suppressed a giggle. Pietro rolled his eyes and nodded to the far wall. 'There's a partition to the kitchen. Camila's been spying on you since you came in.'

Theo glanced behind him as the partition widened and Camila beamed at them. Her gaze rested on Inez. 'Your *feijoadas* are good enough, but I always believed your destiny lies elsewhere.' She blew a kiss and shut the partition.

Pietro left and Theo stared down at her. 'Are you ready to start our adventure, *agape mou*?'

'What does that mean?'

'It means *my love*.' His smile dimmed. 'I learnt to speak Portuguese for the wrong reasons. I will teach you Greek for the right ones.'

Her grip tightened on his shirt. 'Were you really planning to leave Rio?'

'Yes. After I persuaded Benedicto to sign over the company into your and Pietro's names, I was done with that soulless vendetta. The thought that I'd lost you in the process nearly killed me.'

'I...what? You got him to sign over the company to us? Theo, we don't want it!'

'It was your grandfather's, then your mother's. It's right that it should be yours and Pietro's. If you don't really want it, I'm sure you'll find a beneficial way to dispose of it.'

She nodded. 'It would go a long way to help the inner city centre and the *favela* kids.'

'Great, we'll make it happen.'

Her heart contracted as she stared into his warm eyes. 'I love you, Theo. Thank you for coming back for me.'

'I couldn't not return, *anjo*, because without you I'm lost.'

She lifted her face to his and he slanted his mouth over hers in a deep, poignant kiss that brought fresh tears to her eyes.

'We need to talk about these tears,' he said drily, then huffed in irritation as his phone beeped again.

'Your brothers?' she guessed.

'And their wives. Ari wants to know if I'm still alive. Sakis wants to know if he can hire you to design his next oil tanker.'

She laughed. 'And their wives?'

He glanced down at the screen and back at her. 'They want to know if they can start planning our wedding.'

She took the phone, flicked the off switch and slipped it into his back pocket. Gripping his waist, she raised herself on tiptoe and leaned close to his ear.

'We will reply to each one of them in the morning. Right now, I want you to take me back to the boat and make love to me, make me yours again. Is that okay?'

'It's more than okay, my angel. It's what I plan to do for the rest of our lives.'

The look of love and adoration in his eyes as he took her hand and walked her out of the room was forever branded on her heart.

* * * * *

#3297 SHEIKH'S DESERT DUTY
The Chatsfield
by Maisey Yates

Sheikh Zayn Al-Ahmar must stop journalist Sophie from destroying his world—so he kidnaps her! But soon Sophie's delectable company puts everything he values at risk. Only one mistress can rule Zayn's heart—will it be Sophie, or his duty?

#3298 THE SECRET HIS MISTRESS CARRIED
by Lynne Graham

Billie fought hard to heal her broken heart after Gio Letsos married someone else. When he storms back into her life, she's determined not to fall for his seduction again. Especially because she has a secret to protect...their son.

#3299 NINE MONTHS TO REDEEM HIM
by Jennie Lucas

I gave Edward St. Cyr my body, which he wanted, and my heart, which he didn't. Did I make a major mistake? Maybe when he knows about our baby it will heal his heart so he can love us both...

#3300 TO SIN WITH THE TYCOON
Seven Sexy Sins
by Cathy Williams

Gabriel Cabrera can get *anything* he wants...until he meets PA Alice Morgan. So he'll draw her to him, his every touch sinfully seductive. And sweet, virginal Alice will come to him willingly so Gabriel can claim his prize...

#3301 FONSECA'S FURY
Billionaire Brothers
by Abby Green

The last time Luca Fonseca saw Serena DePiero, he'd ended up in a jail cell. So when he discovers she's working for *his* charity, his anger reignites. Serena can handle anything...except the passion that flares hotter than Luca's fury.

#3302 INHERITED BY HER ENEMY
by Sara Craven

As the final words of Virginia Mason's stepfather's will are read, her innocent life suddenly shatters. With no inheritance, her future—and her family's—is entirely in the hands of enigmatic and outrageously attractive Frenchman Andre Duchard.

#3303 THE RUSSIAN'S ULTIMATUM
by Michelle Smart

Emily Richardson has Pascha Virshilas's private documents to blackmail him into clearing her father's name...but Pascha has his own terms. Emily must accompany him to his private island, where the wind blows aside suspicions to reveal something much more dangerous—lust!

#3304 THE LAST HEIR OF MONTERRATO
by Andie Brock

Rafael Revaldi needs an heir, but first he must win back his estranged wife! Lottie returns to the castle she once called home, but can she risk her heart again to give them the child they both so desperately want?

REQUEST YOUR FREE BOOKS!

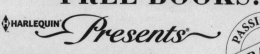

HARLEQUIN *Presents*

PASSION GUARANTEED SEDUCTION

2 FREE NOVELS PLUS
2 FREE GIFTS!

YES! Please send me 2 FREE Harlequin Presents® novels and my 2 FREE gifts (gifts are worth about $10). After receiving them, if I don't wish to receive any more books, I can return the shipping statement marked "cancel." If I don't cancel, I will receive 6 brand-new novels every month and be billed just $4.30 per book in the U.S. or $4.99 per book in Canada. That's a saving of at least 14% off the cover price! It's quite a bargain! Shipping and handling is just 50¢ per book in the U.S. and 75¢ per book in Canada.* I understand that accepting the 2 free books and gifts places me under no obligation to buy anything. I can always return a shipment and cancel at any time. Even if I never buy another book, the two free books and gifts are mine to keep forever.   106/306 HDN FVRK

Name _____ (PLEASE PRINT)

Address _____ Apt. #

City _____ State/Prov. _____ Zip/Postal Code

Signature (if under 18, a parent or guardian must sign)

Mail to the **Harlequin® Reader Service:**
IN U.S.A.: P.O. Box 1867, Buffalo, NY 14240-1867
IN CANADA: P.O. Box 609, Fort Erie, Ontario L2A 5X3

**Are you a current subscriber to Harlequin Presents books
and want to receive the larger-print edition?
Call 1-800-873-8635 or visit www.ReaderService.com.**

* Terms and prices subject to change without notice. Prices do not include applicable taxes. Sales tax applicable in N.Y. Canadian residents will be charged applicable taxes. Offer not valid in Quebec. This offer is limited to one order per household. Not valid for current subscribers to Harlequin Presents books. All orders subject to credit approval. Credit or debit balances in a customer's account(s) may be offset by any other outstanding balance owed by or to the customer. Please allow 4 to 6 weeks for delivery. Offer available while quantities last.

Your Privacy—The Harlequin® Reader Service is committed to protecting your privacy. Our Privacy Policy is available online at www.ReaderService.com or upon request from the Harlequin Reader Service.

We make a portion of our mailing list available to reputable third parties that offer products we believe may interest you. If you prefer that we not exchange your name with third parties, or if you wish to clarify or modify your communication preferences, please visit us at www.ReaderService.com/consumerschoice or write to us at Harlequin Reader Service Preference Service, P.O. Box 9062, Buffalo, NY 14269. Include your complete name and address.

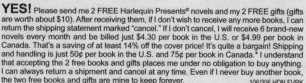

HP13